LI'T
SHARK

CONTENT

Dear readers, we always want to support you and give you the information you need to have the best reading experience possible. Please note that Issue 8 is our SHARK WEEK issue for the year, and true to Shark Week and other similar documentary materials, there are troubling elements in this collection, including animal violence, hunting, pollution, and animal extinction, as well as death, mental health issues, illusions to child loss, and animal death. There are multiple illusions to sexual activity and expletives. Thank you again for your support. We hope you will enjoy our eighth issue, our final issue of 2024.

COPYRIGHT

Copyright © 2024 by Lit Shark Magazine. All rights reserved. No part of this publication may be reproduced, distributed, or transmitted in any form or by any means, including photocopying, recording, or other electronic or mechanical methods, without the prior written permission of the publisher, except as permitted by U.S. copyright law. For permission requests, contact McKenzie Lynn Tozan at Lit Shark Magazine.

The stories, poems, all names, characters, and incidents portrayed in this production are fictitious. No identification with actual persons (living or deceased), places, buildings, and products is intended or should be inferred.

Editor-in-Chief: McKenzie Lynn Tozan
Book Cover and Interior Design: McKenzie Lynn Tozan
Works By: Various Writers (credited)
Cover Image By: Fuvah Mulah Dive School
Cover Spine Image By: Slaveika Aladjova
First Edition 2024

LITERARY MAGAZINE • ISSUE NO. 8 • NOV 2024

LIT SHARK
magazine

THE **SHARK WEEK** EDITION

EDITED BY MCKENZIE LYNN TOZAN

SOMETHING TO SINK YOUR TEETH INTO

LETTER FROM THE EDITOR

Hi readers, writers, and shark fans!

I am so incredibly excited for *Issue 8 of Lit Shark Magazine: The SHARK WEEK Edition*. We were originally going to release this issue earlier this year, but when submissions were a little lower than usual, we decided to extend our creation of this issue, and I'm so grateful we took a chance on it and waited, because I could not be happier with the resulting issue!

Lit Shark is meant to be an inclusive, creative, and accessible community for writers of all backgrounds, but it's also supposed to be an accessible space for information and education centering around marine life, conservation, restoration, and of course, destigmatizing the portrayal of sharks in the media. Since the beginning, I knew that Lit Shark would offer a nod to *SHARK WEEK* each year, because I know how much fun that week is for many shark lovers, and it's also a key time to educate viewers and readers about the real demeanor of sharks. I imagined having a *SHARK WEEK* issue each year that would serve as a literary extension of that week, but that it would be open to interpretation: writers could respond to something from SHARK WEEK, another documentary, their own experiences, and their minds. Just like our *Spooky (TEETH) Edition* this year, our writers did not disappoint with their interpretations of the prompt once they had a little more time to submit!

What resulted was an incredible selection of fiction, short memoirs, photography, and primarily poetry, and the work centers around our connections with nature through experiences with all of our senses, marine life, destigmatizing sharks and other similar animals, and experiencing a general awe at the world around us.

The works in this collection are unique and thoughtful, viscerally image-driven, in conversation with great contemporary poets, and beautifully memorable. The pieces in this collection are a lovely portrayal of literature and quality writing while also performing a wonderful examination of the natural world. This is a collection I envision myself turning back to time and time again when I need a moment in the world, by the seaside, or in an idyllic cliffside community, hearing the calls of gulls and gannets, and trying my luck at seeing a whale breach.

As always, I hope you feel the passion that went into these pages, both from this issue's writers and from the person who curated and designed them. I hope this issue will call up beautiful memories from past summers and will carry through to next spring.

Happy Reading! Until Issue 9,
McKenzie
Editor-in-Chief and Fellow Shark Fan
November 2024

CONTENTS

Letter from the Editor: Shark Week   04

ONE: SHARK WEEK

More Than Bone - KB Ballentine	13
Whale - Noland Blain	14
Piglet Squid - Christa Fairbrother	15
Bottom Feeder - Tonnie Richmond	16
Collective Mind of Small Fish - Nicky Carter	17
Ocean Haiku Sequence - Christiana Doucette	18
In Deep - Michele Rule	19
"lanky gray face (for perfect days surfing lincoln city) - Mike Sluchinski	20
Whose Lake Is This - Michael O. Zahn	22
Bull Male Sleeping - Abigail Ottley	24
Jaws Wide Open (photograph) - Carlin McCarthy	25
"Tokitae" - Catherine Puma	26

TWO: BEAUTIFUL CREATURES

There Is a Beautiful Creature . . . - Carolyn Martin	31
Beauty Rusts without Use - Alan Cohen	32
Wildflower Pilgrimage, Great Smokies - Diana Woodcock	33
Questions about the Sea - Kiki Adams	34
What Is It the Heron Can Teach Me? - Mark Strohschein	36
With Thanks - Carolyn Martin	38

THREE: CHILDHOOD ROSES

Overhead - Ursula McCabe	43
Look Up, Down, All Around - Ursula McCabe	44
Picking Roses as a Child - Lynette G. Esposito	45
Last Pick - Doug Van Hooser	46
Heaven Is a Garden in Essex - Abigail Ottley	49
Where I Grew Up - Beth Kanell	50
Yuki's Eggnog Delight - Michael Shoemaker	51
Gulf Shores - Lisa Nanette Allender	52
Repetition - Annette Gagliardi	54
Glacial Lullaby - Diana Woodcock	55

FOUR: ROCKY WATERS

Finding My New Normal - Chris Wood	59
Loneliness Is a Hungry Bird - Julian Matthews	60
Tarnished - Megan Cartwright	62
Empty Beach - Edward Ahern	63
Elegy for the Great Pacific Garbage Patch - Isaac Fox	64
Recycle - Helga Kidder	66
God Gulped When the Gun Went Off - Beth Kanell	67
We Learned It from YOU - Rie Sheridan Rose	68
Rock - Peter Kay	75
My Words Slip - Annette Gagliardi	77
Surface Tension - Carol Edwards	78
Ode to Loneliness - David Dephy	80
Three Part Poem - Dale E. Cottingham	82
silent soliloquy: contemplation of rediscovery & grievance. - S. Abdulwasi'h Olaitan	84
Beached - Janina Aza Karpinska	85
Tale of the Twin Red Oaks - Chris Wood	86
To My Father from a New Climate - Dale E. Cottingham	87
what spoiled this poem is the alarm of loss - S. Abdulwasi'h Olaitan	89
Stoking Hope's Last Ember - Diana Woodcock	91

FIVE: THE CRIME OF EXISTING

Turning Turtle - Abigail Ottley	95
Lost - Roy Adams	96
Poem on a Few Lines of Billy Collins's *Whale Day* - D.C. Buschmann	97
Mud Devil or Angel? - Diana Woodcock	98
Sanctuary of Voices - Mark Strohschein	100
Pain is a Shark - Christa Fairbrother	102
Cicadas Hatching - Beth Kanell	103
Earthing - Chris Wood	104
Maligned Mother - Amber Sayer	105
Elegy for One Thousand-Plus Manatees - Diana Woodcock	107
Infidelity - Beth Marquez	109
The Last Bee - Julian Matthews	110
The Last Jellyfish - Dustin Brown	112
The Crime of Existing - Zenia deHaven	113

SIX: CLIMATE CHANGE

Winter - Dale E. Cottingham	123
Rain's Ensemble - Ursula McCabe	124
The Sea Serpent - Christiana Doucette	126

Headwinds - David Dephy	127
Forced - Lauren K. Nixon	128
With Whale Sharks - Diana Woodcock	129
Storm Petrel - Lauren K. Nixon	131

SEVEN: BIRDS OF THE AIR

Meadowlark, Walt, Me - GTimothy Gordon	135
It's Singles Day in the 'Burbs - Lauren K. Nixon	136
Heron Rises - Mark Strohschein	138
Second Brood - Doug Van Hooser	139
Mornings - Ursula McCabe	140
Gannet - Tonnie Richmond	141
Gull - J.S. Watts	142
Water Sounds - Lauren K. Nixon	143
Resilience, In Theory - Beth Kanell	144
"Frogs on a green leaf . . ." - Lynette G. Esposito	145
Dreamtime, I Will Song - KB Ballentine	146

EIGHT: KINGDOM BY THE SEA

Gardening in Astoria - Ursula McCabe	151
Along the Strand - Lorraine Caputo	152
Testament of the Naiad of Little Beck, Baildon - Lauren K. Nixon	153
The Oyster - Gregg Norman	154
Breakfast on the Boat - Gregg Norman	155
Cream Puff, le Magnifique - Michael Shoemaker	156
Mull Head, Deerness 2022 - Tonnie Richmond	157
Wetlands - Jim Wolper	158
Dare Not Blink - Diana Woodcock	159

NINE: TIME TO GIVE BACK

Today's Morning - Ursula McCabe	163
Variations on 'Joy is Not Made to Be a Crumb' - Doug Van Hooser	164
Nightlight - GTimothy Gordon	165
What a Poet Desires - Carolyn Martin	166
Lioconcha hieroglyphica - Noland Blain	167
Kelp Forest - Diana Woodcock	168

Acknowledgements	173
About Our Contributors: Bios	177
Submit to Lit Shark and Write for Us: Info	195

On August 8, 1970, a large-scale attempt to round up orcas to display in marine parks went horribly wrong in Penn Cove, Washington. With the use of speed boats, explosives, and spotter planes, 80 orcas were forcefully herded into the area. Seven of their calves were captured, and another five were drowned in nets and unnaturally sunk to conceal their deaths. One of the seven calves taken was Tokitae, also known as Lolita, who lived in captivity as a performer at Miami Seaquarium for the next five decades. She died in 2023, just months before she was supposed to be released.

On November 4, 2024, more than 50 years after the attack, Tokitae's pod, tracked as "L Pod" and consisting of 34 orcas, traveled home to Penn Cove for the very first time. As whales have long memories and also pass generational knowledge, including dangerous territories, to their offspring, their return is nothing short of awe-inspiring and hope-inducing.

This issue is for them.

To Tokitae, Lolita . . . they made it home.
Rest in peace, light, and calm waters, sweet one.

ONE:
SHARK WEEK

KB BALLENTINE

MORE THAN BONE

This sea, this salt,
this very wind is part of me.
   Orange and pink swirl
      the horizon just before
    a half-sun pulls itself into a sky
   wide with gulls and pelicans.
Oystercatchers dance
       between water and sand—
    each drop and grain a part of me,
       my breath.
Palm trees sing
      of wind and wave—
   moon fading.
A part of me, shadows of dunes
    and marram grass scrape the edge
      of my vision. A sighing
somewhere inside me reaching for home.

NOLAND BLAIN

WHALE

Listen: there is another language beneath our own.
I saw its raised fin, its huge umbral body slick
against the ocean surface. Just then, a wet, new verb
thrust out of the water like—oh I don't know,
the ancestor of *breathe*. The first form of *open*.

You and I can wipe our mouths and pronounce
the same syllables, going *bar bar bar*
until the bicycle unmangles or the moon unflattens:
our nouns the worst possible nouns, the *thwop*
of the fish against the dock and never

the animal itself. Someday, go out with me,
onto the sea, and if in good faith we watch the waves
crest and froth into unreadable syntax, then eventually,
the chatter will get quiet. If only for a few seconds.
Then I can try again. To tell you what I mean.

CHRISTA FAIRBROTHER

PIGLET SQUID

Squid can communicate differently
on each side of their bodies, one side fight—
speckled, violent sparks. One side love—shy
gentle pulses. At the aquarium
I learn my chronic illness makes me a
squid, one side healthy, one side sick. The left
side, always the left. When my skin speckles
hot red, my eye twitches, movement becomes
slow motion. Change my shape, camouflage to
pretend nothing's wrong. Look, if you hold still
you can just see. Secretly, the juicy,
jelly soft parts, all of me, wants to be
scooped up and held, bathed in your tenderness.
Love is said to be bright, luminescent.

TONNIE RICHMOND

BOTTOM FEEDER

Things fall down here. Food. Rubbish.
I can tell the difference.
Fragments of flesh, bones, and the finer sauce
of plankton and dead krill. All for me.

The water in these depths is black, opaque.
I don't care, my eyes don't work.
I use my nose to see, sniff out the tasty morsels.
Whale blubber, fish scales, human toes. Delicious.

I try hard to spit out the tiny bits
of indigestible stuff that fall with the food
these days. Hard, nasty flakes, get into my gills.
Human-made, they say. Indestructible.

NICKY CARTER

Honorable Mention for Lit Shark's September 2024 Poem of the Month

COLLECTIVE MIND OF SMALL FISH

I might have drifted off   drifted out forgotten
I could breathe through ears swivel eyes
fins above in front behind   hidden in fish-us

roll through wreck-depths   rise
through a warm feast of tiny things
didn't know they could taste so good

where fish-us goes   big fish follow
but they don't roll   as one
get picked off   by harpoon birds

dropping from the blue-grey dome
one   pierces fish-us   misses
and we reform   bounce off backs

of demon dolphins   they don't roll
they twitter and chatter-snap at big fish
round them up   take their fill

blubber-bull-seal hunts alone   comes at fish-us fast
we separate   as his whiskers brush us
fish-us   has met him before

trawler men   last in the queue
they don't trouble the thoughts of fish-us
we roll through holes   in giant nets

but   I worry I upset them once
another tide   a different sky   I drift onshore
a lost   and solitary   baitfish

already missing my collective mind

CHRISTIANA DOUCETTE

OCEAN HAIKU SEQUENCE

Sitting on the tube
we avoid the breakers rush
between the waves

These schools keep current
surfing streams for the closest
weekend manatee

Sea lions back him into
the corner, seal the deal
with a net gain.

A whale as he spouts.
others leap away air pods
breeching the silence.

Fish for compliments
claiming all the anemones
orange clown's coral.

Finally clams up
all the waiting gulls
flock forward

Ocean marathon
close chums keep pace, then coast
to a shark fin-ish.

MICHELE RULE

Honorable Mention for Lit Shark's July-August 2024 Poem of the Month

IN DEEP

Out on the ocean
neon yellow kayak.

Scared of the water
even crystal blue.
Can't swim,
hate getting my face wet.
But still
here because I wonder.

This far out
from rolling dunes
grittiness of sand.
What might be down there?

Flashlight fish.
Cookiecutter sharks.
Bristlemouths. Anglerfish.
Viperfish.

These names don't make me feel better.
Sharp teeth, pointy spines, luring, blinking lights.
I'm a land creature,
born of fir trees and black peat
roots and lungs.

Yet born
with curiousity,
crawling and extending
past my fear and forward.

MIKE SLUCHINSKI

LANKY GRAY FACE
(FOR PERFECT DAYS SURFING
LINCOLN CITY)

the things i like to think about
when i'm floating deep
blue colors and there's
black no bottom or just kelp forests
dug deep somewhere down
i like to think about the
ocean and the land
and those shore types
and their own fears and
mystical beings and then
some talk about wolves and
the spirit animals and some
cry wolf and they thought they
saw something some lanky
gray face and others laugh
those who did and cried wolf
but when i'm sitting on my
board out there freezing under
a wetsuit thick blubber
black rubber
no one near the place
lincoln city or along the oregon coast
no one not even the canadians
think about crying shark

there's no words for it
and no one wants to catch
not even a glimpse
of a lanky gray face
teeth first grins
or a fin rising
out of the waves

MICHAEL O. ZAHN

WHOSE LAKE IS THIS

> *"Property owners bordering a lake have property rights in the lake itself."*
> —"Water Rights in Florida"

Whose lake this is, I think I know:
The residents who swim below
or ride the pulsing winds that blow
and stir the waves where others ride
and rustle weeds where sly ones lurk
(and shy ones hide)

Whose lake this is, I think I know—
we see their spoor
and hear their caws and croaks,
their screeches, hoots and grunts and growls,
their pants and burps and barks and howls
(beware their hisses and their snarls)

Whose lake this is, I think I know:
Creatures who possess no title,
no paper trail, no deed on file.
Though the lake's their domicile,
they cannot claim their rights at trial.

They cannot swear an oath
in court of law
by raising fin or wing or paw.
Their testimony goes unheard
for lack of speech, for lack of word.

Yet...

Their ownership's
no mystery—
their presence
precedes history.
(But lawyers wearing wingtip shoes
sidestep clients who pee and poop
wherever they choose.)

ABIGAIL OTTLEY

BULL MALE SLEEPING

Despite my glazed, black eye, not dead, not I.
A whaling man would know better.

A kittiwake spoke and by the power of my flukes
I heaved my scarred bulk at the the sky.

Now blow-hole to the surface I am perpendicular,
at peace with my own slap and wallow.

Between the music that lulls me and the tide's sharp tug
slides the shadow of the she-whale who suckled me.

How perfectly we swam, my smaller belly nudging hers.
I learned worship at the altar of her mouth.

Now time makes me master of this brooding estate.
Only Man and great Orca oppose me.

My desire is to swim. I will father many children.
My purpose is to breech and blow.

JAWS WIDE OPEN

—Carlin McCarthy

CATHERINE PUMA

"TOKITAE"

Come home, come home,
where your mother waits for you in the Salish Sea.

Stolen baby, kept in captivity;
half a century in a tank
more shallow than you were long,
the smallest cage for your kind.

You child performer,
you profitable commodity.
We whistle and yell,
Splash for us, beg for your food!

Come home, come home,
for death has finally freed you.

The red tape fell away when your life ended.
We cut you open, you blackfish,
dissecting our fellow mammal.
The necropsy says renal failure.

It is cheaper to transport a dead whale than a live one.
Your remains cremated and ashes returned
to the Lummi Nation, your kin on land.
Three decades of advocacy at an end.

Come home, come home,
where your family gathers on your day of death.

You belong in the deep
seas of ancestry,
where your lineage still sings
the lullabies from your infancy.

May your spirit follow the currents
and sink into fathoms of early memory,
when you rolled and played in the wild
where the Chinook leapt in the cold sea spray.

TWO:
BEAUTIFUL CREATURES

CAROLYN MARTIN

Winner of Lit Shark's July-August 2024 Poem of the Month

THERE IS A BEAUTIFUL CREATURE...

> *"There is a beautiful creature living in a hole you have dug."*
> —Hafiz, "Beautiful Creature"

Put the shovel down
and slide your hands
into dark earth.
With the finesse
of an archeologist,
brush off each deep-down bone
that held the you of you.
Look for secrets
the cranium hid.
Bless the breaths born
in sternum and ribs.
Praise the moving grace
of femurs and tibia.
Check off the list.
Then cradle them all
with gratitude.
Find the creature
they esteemed.
Fall in love.
She grew beautiful.

ALAN COHEN

BEAUTY RUSTS WITHOUT USE

We would find it in unlikeliness
The wind blowing
The sky alive with desperate leaves

But just then
We might be looking down
A fallen wreath

Some needles scattered
A hawk, unnoticed, overhead
We sweep them onto a pan
Empty them into our dustbin

Only we can use it
Beauty
Why else are we here?

DIANA WOODCOCK

Honorable Mention for Lit Shark's November 2024 Poem of the Month

WILDFLOWER PILGRIMAGE, GREAT SMOKIES

Such astounding biodiversity
in this unbroken chain of peaks
on this fifth largest planet
third from the sun.

                        Everything alive,
                        catching storing releasing
                        energy, all those little buds
                        hidden in dark winter,

waiting till now to burst
upon the scene.
What I would give
to be the giddy bee

                        about the clover, or tiger
                        swallowtail, or hummingbird
                        come to dine on the trumpetvine.
                        Or the guardian angel watching

over the endangered ones
exposed to air pollution,
off-trail hiking, poaching
(orchids, trilliums, gingseng).

                        Lyrical, intoxicating,
                        inviting the pilgrim to flee
                        the unnatural, unholy world
                        and dwell for a spell with

            Mother Nature among her flowers.

KIKI ADAMS

QUESTIONS ABOUT THE SEA

When you lie on your back
in the sunshine, you can feel the pattern
of light dancing through water ripples.

They say a person (while alive)
is a wave riding on a vast ocean,
the illusion of separation.

But if you and I are water from one sea,
what fish live in that sea?

Do ribbons of color chase
each other through the gentle

shadows and sunspots of an endless
reef that is the comfort of home?

Do angelfish circle, laughing
at the shapes they have been given?

Are there ancient sharks lurking
off the cliffs, waiting for a feeling

of envy or greed in the shape
of a damselfish to stray too close?

Are the fish kept company
by forests of primordial jellies,

pods of whales singing that haunting
harmony our souls remember,

or squid so huge they swallow suns,
black holes freed from physics?

Do sea turtles ferry worlds
through plankton stars?

If phantom ships could sail that sea,
what gods would be captain and crew?

Would storms come to overturn them,
or tentacles reaching from the deep?

Do you remember the saltwater embrace
we gave as the last captain fell

through eternity to our hungry fish below?

MARK STROHSCHEIN

WHAT IS IT THE HERON CAN TEACH ME?

I.

necessity of blank-slate days

II.

appreciate movement
but ally with stillness

III.

raw obedience to patience

IV.

we hide behind safety of glass

V.

beauty & majesty

VI.

the quiet
the space between the quiet

VII.

this life-affirming
retreat inward

VIII.

how to be a mere stich
in king-sized tapestry of life

CAROLYN MARTIN

WITH THANKS

You do not have to be a tiger
wandering lonely in a misty dawn
or a patient spider curating its craft
in a sun-sprinkled maple tree or the fog
that creeps into any month that is not cruel.

Rather, be a hot and holy seller of truth
with more than thirteen ways of looking.
Offer homage to magic hips and Flanders Fields,
to the Jabberwock, Albatross, and slouching beast.
And don't forget attention must be paid
to those who go gently every night.

It comes down to this: Wisdom tilts the world
toward love, and life is a grain of sand,
a taken road, a stage playing out a tragi-comedy.
And, maybe, a fourteenth look will glimpse
a primal Whimper searching for creation's Bang,
or the primal Bang curious to see what it's become.

THREE: CHILDHOOD ROSES

URSULA MCCABE

OVERHEAD

Overhead I hear
the guttural sounds,
I'm stopped in my tracks
by their musical honks.

The big breasted
birds fly over in a V shape,
sky's attempt at cursive handwriting.

So often there is a laggard,
a lone bird that straggles,
the honk a moan, a wailing call-
I'm alone, being left behind.

I remember my stepfather
teaching me to shoot,
brace for the recoil, my ten-year-old
shoulders would stiffen up.

I didn't tell him I'd never hunt,
I'd never aim for a deer's dun hide,
or the rosy chest of a duck.

The geese are gone now,
searching for their next refuge.

How I miss that man,
the way he made us a family again.
For him to be my father,
we didn't have to share
blood at all.

URSULA MCCABE

LOOK UP, DOWN, ALL AROUND

Swatches of light filter on
this farmland trail,
green first, then blue,
onward straight through
to where more oaks live.

Above comes a drumming sound,
rat-a-tat-tat,
his rolled-up tongue reaches for sap,
sapsucker creeps round a large tree trunk.

I dodge cow pies,
and look for flattened shapes in the
deep grass where deer slept,
their legs tucked.

LYNETTE G. ESPOSITO

PICKING ROSES AS A CHILD

The thorns do not care

the child is innocent.

Let it learn as it cries

and sucks its finger

from the pain . . . blood.

The roses hang their heads

In shame—their stems in a cool

water-filled vase.

They should have known the mother

would come and teach

the little one to use the pruners.

Oh what they would do for an aspirin.

DOUG VAN HOOSER

LAST PICK

Zeke had spent much of the day under the porch trying to catch one of the farm's six kittens. Crawling over the myriad of two by fours supporting the structure, choking on his self-made dust cloud, the mother cat hissing and swinging a thorned paw at him at least a dozen times. Zeke's mom scolded him as she tried to knock dirt from his clothes, shook her head, and cleaned his glasses. Zeke's one eye floated up to the left. The glasses' prescription incorrect, meant to try and strengthen the drifting eye's muscles.

Daylight was dimming as shouts and laughter filled dusk's umbrella. The adults all inside the house drinking coffee, embellishing stories. The yearly reunion had a way of resizing memories. The kids outside in the large front yard playing Marco Polo, then a game of *tag, you're it*. Kids, like the fireflies, were here then disappeared, darting from a corner of the yard to an opposite edge or circling the yard like a flushed commode. Tiffany, Zeke and Jefferson's five-year old sister, bobbed up and down as she pleaded with first one cousin then another to tag her and make her *it*. But it was Zeke the older kids tagged over and again. Viewed as the weak link, his eyeglasses askew, a thin reed in any wind, but determined and relentless as a dog playing fetch. Undaunted by scrapes, scratches, and grass stains, his will to compete resolute.

Jefferson, who wouldn't answer to Jeff, stood at the top of the porch steps. The oldest kid acting as an adult overseeing the games. Calling out instructions and rules, he saved Zeke the first time by saying a person could not be *it* again until three others had been. The second time he ended the game by calling for a relay race. Five-man teams the four oldest cousins picked in a round robin draft. Jefferson picking last. Quickly, the boys and older girls were chosen, followed by the ten, eleven and twelve-year-old kids, then the next three years younger, Zeke's category. Picked last by his brother to no one's surprise.

It was dark now and fireflies dotted the air. The contestants would start directly in front of the porch steps where the next person would be tagged into the race. The course ran out and around the old hand water pump their grandfather still drank from and drew water for the dogs and flowers. Then out and around a large oak stump, home to Cornbread, the six-foot corn snake. Then to the edge of the farm's yard where Hilda, the eight-foot tall, six-foot wide shrub rose, was in full bloom. Her sweet scent perfuming the cooling night air. Then back to the touch-in point in front of the porch.

Jefferson gathered his four teammates. They huddled with their arms slung over each other's shoulders. The plan was simple. Fifteen-year old Tommie would go first, an attempt to get into the lead. Followed by Darlene, who had spent the last six months struggling with puberty, then Dennis, a loud-mouth ten-year old who took delight in teasing everyone but mostly Zeke. Jefferson put his finger in Zeke's chest and told him, "You're fourth. Do your best to keep it close so I have a shot at passing whoever's ahead of us."

The water pump was close enough to the house to be seen. The only light in the yard was a small lamp on the opposite side and at the end of the long driveway. Cornbread's stump was at the limit of the lamp's light. Hilda was in the dark at the far side of the yard. The teams' first runners lined up in front of the porch steps. Jefferson raised his arm into the air and dropped it shouting "go!"

Tommie was a good choice and was the first to touch his teammate into the race, but Darlene was quickly overcome as she kept one arm slung across her chest as she ran. Surprisingly, Dennis ran as fast his mouth and the team was close to the lead in third place. He slapped the back of Zeke's head, shouting, "Run Four Eyes!"

Shouts and cheers rose in the dark nighttime air like carillon bells. Zeke's right foot slid on the grass as he took off. He had to put his left hand down to avoid falling. As he rounded the water pump, his foot slipped in the damp grass again. His cousin

Amy passed him. He caught her at Cornbread's corner and shot in front of her, but the two boys in front of him were already halfway to the shrub rose. His heart pounding, he gulped air, "stay close" ringing in his ears as he willed his legs to pump faster. He saw the two boys turn which meant Hilda was straight ahead. He grit his teeth in determination sucking air hard and fast. He looked to see where the other two boys were, thinking faster! Faster! And crashed into the rose bush.

His glasses tore from his face. Hilda's thorns slashing his arms, legs, chest and face. He tried to push himself away from the bush, but the razor bladed branches cut into his hands. He twisted and turned trying to escape, but the rosebush held him, slicing his every movement. His fierce determination could not free him. As he struggled, he whimpered, "Let go! Let go!" the thorns ripping him. Hilda would not release him.

Jefferson watched as the two boys tagged in their teams' final runner. Zeke should be close, but he wasn't. Jefferson had seen Zeke wasn't that far behind. Where was he? Jefferson peered into the dark, and then he heard Zeke's voice, a whine like a lonely dog left tied to a post. He started towards the sound. As he got close, he saw Zeke thrashing in the bush. A sudden shout of "let go!" pierced the shouts and cheers of the other kids. Jefferson stepped to the side as the two cousins ran by, neck and neck.

Zeke was sobbing, trying to punch his way out. Jefferson had to tell him repeatedly, "calm down, calm down, we'll get you out." Finally, once Jefferson got a hand on his shoulder, Zeke quit fighting. "Hold still, man, you're cutting both of us." The cousins slowly became aware something was going on and started to crowd around the bush. Zeke's breath seethed in a loud hiss. The shouts and yells faded. Then Dennis' voice rang out, "Geez, only a cross-eyed dumb ass would run into a rosebush."

It would be another minute before the adults arrived, thanks to five-year old Tiffany. They had to cut Zeke out of the bush. It took five years for Hilda to look like her old self. The taunts and the failure faded over Zeke's many years, but the shrub rose's scent never left him.

ABIGAIL OTTLEY

Winner of Lit Shark's October 2024 Poem of the Month

HEAVEN IS A GARDEN IN ESSEX

Mint and lemon balm grew under the cooking apple tree in Nana's big back garden. You could smell them while you napped on the daisy-dotted lawn in the still-too-warm, three o'clock shade. Bees bumbled there and a family of crows flapped in the leafy upper branches; sometimes a cuckoo came cuck-cuck-calling or a hearty robin foraged for worms. Always, it seemed, there was the faint buzz and drone of a neighbour's new-fangled mower, startling, stopping, starting again, too far away to be seen.

And this is the heaven I carry in my head for those days when the world is too much with me, when the horror, the hurt or sheer awfulness of living escalates to more than I can bear. Because summer stays on here, well into September, and most mornings we go out after windfalls. While Nana makes a hammock from her big blue apron, I sally forth with a basket. I fetch the old wicker one with the roughly mended handles from the glory hole under the stairs.

Most of all, because it is Nana who instructs me I shouldn't be too *picky*; that crows, and even maggots, are also God's creatures and they too must eat. We limit our growth when we set our sights greedily, to harvest only whole and perfect apples: the bruised and fallen fruit is easier to gather; it, too, is wholesome and good.

BETH KANELL

WHERE I GREW UP

The streets had names and lay in parallel—
some planner placed them straight and without views
unless you paid the premium to roost
above the rest, the upper mansions. Swell,

or swollen up with pride? I never knew,
child of a pair of strivers, caught below.
Now, of course, I think (really, I know)
that perching halfway up is useful too.

Aging in a back-road home, I check the sky:
the scudding clouds, the mountains, and the field.
This land wraps routes like cats' tails, gently curled
and tracked at night by deer and bears (oh my!).
So have my loves encircled me. I yield
to how this unplanned place became my world.

MICHAEL SHOEMAKER

YUKI'S EGGNOG DELIGHT

I own a glass mug
No beer goes inside.
Eggnog is its
only draft.

The wild scrounger,
(my cat takes
 no offense)
winds around
brushing my ankles
making figure eights.

I leave my mug
unattended
on the kitchen table
to turn the TV
off in the living room.

When I return
Yuki, my little snowball,
you are submerged
up to your ears
frantically lapping up
eggnog
for the first time
as fast as Santa's
magic reindeer.

Forgive me, for laughing.
I know it is a hard thing
to wait until next Thanksgiving
for eggnog's comeback
to supermarket splendor.

LISA NANETTE ALLENDER

GULF SHORES

I name the manta rays *Larry, Curly,* and *Moe,* an homage to those
Saturday mornings spent watching
The Three Stooges in black and white,
my father laughing, my sister laughing, me laughing,
my mother shaking her head, *I don't think they are funny.*

My mother ridiculed us for watching such slapstick.
It's silly, she would say.
Oh, Mom, it's supposed to be.

Saturday morning cartoons, *Star Trek, Gilligan's Island,*
The Addams Family, The Munsters, these my sister and Dad loved.
And so did I.
They're not realistic, Mom said from our tiny yellow kitchen. She
hovered near our *Harvest Gold* refrigerator, pouring the batter
for pancakes, peeling and juicing the oranges.

But when Barbara Eden danced across the tv screen at the
beginning of *I Dream of Jeannie,* Mom's voice changed.
She called Dad by both his names, sort of.
John R. you don't need to watch that.
Sometimes, on those autumn Sundays when football was on,
she'd stand in front of the tv at half-time, obscuring my Dad's view
of the cheerleaders. *You like the blondes,* she would say.
I never thought Dad preferred blondes.

Today my husband knelt next to me, our knees coated in the sticky sand, and we watched Larry, Curly, and Moe race each other, the water rushing up, foam hovering over them. A floating, furry clump of seaweed which I named *Cousin It,* in memory of the strange, long-haired character on The Addams Family, swished past them, and we laughed. Then my husband chased me down the beach.

The kite I flew, kept swirling, diving, falling.

ANNETTE GAGLIARDI

REPETITION

the pattern of days
that made our lives
is still discernable

at the window
a dog looks out
and barks perpetual news

birds sing their daily song
continuing long into the
evening and beyond

wheeling down the oil-
streaked highway
along the lip of lives lived,

a stain descends—
love descending also
holding life

with the glue that binds,
with the constancy of wind,
with the pattern of days

DIANA WOODCOCK

GLACIAL LULLABY

Here are sounds to both
awaken and lull to sleep:
the falling of a boulder,

the rolling of stones into crevasses
and moraine ridges, a stream
flowing into a glacier well,

the solemn roaring of a torrent
rushing under a glacier's edge,
the popping of air bubbles

being set free, rills whispering,
moulins grinding, brooks
gurgling as they glide into blue

channels—these the sounds
of fluidity, water in motion
from icy heights to depths of ocean.

And the sounds of everything born
in the midst of all this constant
commotion—wolves howling,

marmots chattering, ptarmigans
harshly cracking and chucking—
how they call out like a bell

to awaken, to protect themselves
from a world flowing, calving,
breaking apart piece by piece.

FOUR:
ROCKY WATERS

CHRIS WOOD

FINDING MY NEW NORMAL

Sparrows sing,
just like they sing every morning.

But I am weary,
my soul mourns.
Loss saturates,
bleeds through my skin,
smears everything I touch.

I scale the wall of uncertainty,
                    fall
into the depths of despair.

Stroking,
        kicking,
I follow the bubbles
            upward
toward the surface,
            toward the light.

JULIAN MATTHEWS

LONELINESS IS A HUNGRY BIRD

Come loneliness
Sit beside me
Tell me why you eat at me so
You peck, nibble and gnaw
I would rather you swallow me whole

Like a tiny kingfisher I once saw
take in a flopping frog, almost its size,
down its gullet, legs still kicking–
Do you think you could give me
that honor, to lose myself so completely

inside your golden-orangey belly,
your shiny, cyan-blue plumage, reflecting
sunlight across a calm, windless pond,
a Nat Geo moment in slo-mo—
how tender and beautiful that end would be?

But you are no kingfisher are you?
More sly scavenger than agile hunter
You rather taunt and tease, stalk and creep,
steal into this house of hope, uninvited,
unannounced, bring your cousins

melancholy and misery over, let solitude
have one too many, make bliss drunk
with despondency, allow grief to dominate
and talk way too loud, down bottle after bottle
of your empty promises, wallow in the wretched

heavy air of deeply-felt absences, missing warmth,
pick at my living heart like it was carrion, my emotions raw,
worn and torn, wary and teary, let me bleed out, stripped
and ripped, nail me to a cross of intrusive doubts, overthink
everything and almost yield—but, wait

I shoo you out again, pull away from this phase,
slip under and over the blue haze—reclaim my truth—
and watch your dull-feathered, scrawny form afar,
perched in the shadows, cawing alone,
chewing at your own claws.

MEGAN CARTWRIGHT

TARNISHED

Seal-sleek and lightly tarnished,
you swam eel-like, swelling my sinuses.
More evolved in every way,
a philosopher, you say
(but I know you like the feel of clay).

I lopped the head off a succulent.
Tracked my dirty boots across town.
Say we were never friends.
Say it, hard against my ear.
I will slip my skin, start again.

EDWARD AHERN

EMPTY BEACH

Early morning is the time of absences
and the unsettling of unique presence,
when up and down the churning surf ribbon
only straggled birds and bubbling clams
hold haphazard position in emptiness
and the lone biped, ignored as insignificant,
feels his fusty persona leaching out
on the windblown sand over green water
until the purging reveals a raw loneliness
that must be poulticed with the spit of others.

ISAAC FOX

ELEGY FOR THE GREAT PACIFIC GARBAGE PATCH

white five-gallon bucket, an orchard's logo long worn away, now covered in gooseneck barnacles and bobbing, up, down, up, down

yellow hardhat, once worn by a man who helped excavate my neighbor's inground pool

green T9 flip-flop, brought here by way of coastal currents, colossal rivers, channelized city streams, frog-filled ditches, and the grinning three-year-old who flung it out the window of her parents' minivan

Styrofoam brick that used to be part of a cooler, crumbling into thousands and thousands of tiny plastic crumbs that will drift under the surface for thousands and thousands of years

sperm whale emerging from the black depths, fed, to take a sip of air

lost nylon fishing net containing:
38 crabs
1 nearly dead juvenile whitetip shark
423 fish skeletons, various species

toilet seat from a small coastal home that was shredded to its foundation by a tsunami

submerged cloud of microplastics so dense, so white, it looks like a snowstorm underwater

coffee cups, milk jugs, water bottles, more than anyone could ever use in one lifetime

previously undiscovered species of crustacean—delicate, green, perfectly camouflaged inside a Mountain Dew bottle

plastic plastic plastic plastic plastic plastic plastic Plastic Plastic PLASTIC PLASTIC PLASTIC PLASTIC PLASTIC PLASTIC PLASTIC **PLASTIC PLASTIC PLASTIC PLASTIC PLAS—**

HELGA KIDDER

RECYCLE

Caught in the down-fall of doom,
I think of the fridge
where food dies:
a passel of leeks wilted,
a pint of strawberries shrunken
and festering mold, lettuce
browning, leaves shriveling.

Where is the food fairy
throwing her mantle of mercy
over the frigid vault?

Where are the gnomes guarding
the produce, fighting
the spoilers, slimers, mushers?

Sulphurous odor and dank stench
attack me, angel of compassion,
as I open the sealed door.

Throw out the rotten food.
Carry it to the compost
where the earth can reclaim
what it so valiantly put forth.

BETH KANELL

GOD GULPED WHEN THE GUN WENT OFF

Three more dead in a hateful shooting, another
dreadful moment in the news cycle: horror, flowers,
mothers grim and grieving.

What use are "thoughts and prayers" now?

Minutes later, my phone buzzed: A new neighbor
who'd armed himself against the wilderness had just shot
an invading porcupine, multiple times before it yielded.
He called to say that killing it, facing its squeals and pain
sickened him. "I won't ever again."

Holy One, send porcupines into the city streets:
more barbed spines, tough hearts,
unbearable cries.

RIE SHERIDAN ROSE

WE LEARNED IT FROM YOU

Pain dominated my life. I don't tell you this to garner sympathy; you must understand this point to understand my story. This controlling fact led to everything else. Every moment of every day brought agony. As a result, I rarely slept the night through. I napped whenever I had a modicum of relief, but even the vaunted opiates made little difference.

So, I guess, in retrospect, the fact I encountered the Visarons before anyone else isn't so surprising. They arrived in a single ship in the dead hours of night when respectable people slept, and the less respectable weren't watching the skies.

I, however, had given up on sleep as the throes of a particularly grueling grocery list of pain and suffering refused to remove its claws from my brain. At that moment, sitting on the back porch with a glass of bourbon and an oxy chaser, I wouldn't have minded if it killed me. At least I would have died happy, and—hopefully—pain-free for a moment.

Of course, the combo wasn't having the desired effect on me, but at least it dulled the pain a bit. As I sat and twitched, searching for the elusive comfortable position, I thought I saw a shooting star arc across the sky. But the object appeared too bright for that explanation. Too close in its trajectory. The something descended in the woods behind my house.

I listened hard, but no boom resounded, no crashing sound. It appeared it had come down under its own power. Since it provided a welcome distraction, I decided I should go investigate the matter. Death was the worst-case scenario, but would that be so terrible?

I picked up my cane, chugged the last of the bourbon, and limped into the woods through the back fence. The stars were thick in the sky, surrounding a full moon. The sparse woods—more haphazard squirrel plantings than actual forest—made the path easy to follow, despite the late hour.

A high-pitched whine, like a giant mosquito, needled its way into my head, getting louder as I got closer to a glow, which I assumed to be my quarry. I rounded a corner of the path and gasped at the sight before me. The object appeared globular, though the bottom of the arc had embedded itself in the soft ground. If the ball had slipped off a mace and chain—only twenty feet in diameter and glowing—it could have been what lay there in the wood.

Without confirmation, I assumed the object was a ship as it continued to whine while I limped around its perimeter. As I circled, the illumination surrounding the thing blinked. Individual spikes flashed on and off, creating a complex ripple pattern.

I stepped back, almost losing my balance, jaw dropping as the whine rose in pitch and a section of the exterior melted away. A gaping hole appeared, filled with a blue light. I admit it—I grew up on *Doctor Who* and *Star Trek*. Something alien had landed in my backyard. Of course, I was going to explore it. After all, I had nothing significant to lose.

Creeping forward, I stepped across the threshold into the interior of the ship. A single, round space met my eye. The ship appeared to have crashed, with its controls somewhat buried in the ground. Two pilot chairs hung suspended in mid-air. The "floor" was relative, as I realized I walked on the curved outer wall surface.

Heart in my throat, I shuffled forward, not daring to break contact with the wall, floor, whatever aspect I stepped on. Both suspended chairs held occupants. Biting my lip, I moved close enough that I could reach out and touch the nearer chair.

A harness, not unlike a child's car seat, held each inert

creature in place. I studied the visitors. One wore a plain green jumpsuit and the other a more ornate gold jumpsuit; both looked the size of a five-year-old. Their skin exhibited a natural gray hue—I guess the movies were right about that—but their eyes appeared normal size. Each had three of them arranged in a triangle.

The one in the green jumpsuit had thick silver hair cut close to the scalp, while the one in gold wore a mass of complicated black braids. I assumed the one in green was male and the gold female based on human stereotypes.

Who were they? Why were they here? Were they dangerous? Should I call someone?

While I considered my options, the one in green stirred and groaned. The sound startled me, and I stumbled backward into the wall. The creature's eyes snapped open, all three turning my way. They glowed with an inner luminosity. The color seemed to shift between green and brown.

Hwkt so enon te? (I recreate its speech as closely as possible, but I never learned their language to be sure the transcription is accurate.) The voice—though inaudible—seemed feminine in tone, and I revised my conceptions.

I heard the alien's words telepathically, but I didn't understand what it wanted.

"I-I don't understand you," I replied with a helpless shrug.

Jfmr nrskes grendstd. The alien gave an audible sigh, and its brow furrowed. "Inglesh?" it said, voice raspy and grating. Its meaning came through clear enough.

I nodded. "English. Yes. You know our language?"

"Some. Not well. Where is?"

"Well, in the general sense, you have landed . . . or, I guess, *crashed* on the planet Earth. Specifically, in Solamente, Texas. I guess someone in the Founding Fathers had a sense of humor." I realized nonsense babbled out of my mouth, but I'd never spoken with an alien before, and I wasn't sure of the protocol. Still, I shut up to be safe.

The second pilot stirred now, then jerked awake. Unquestionable panic flashed across its face. The first alien spoke in a comforting tone to its partner. I couldn't understand a word of their odd language, but it seemed to calm the other down.

Turning back to face me, the first alien said, "I am designated Xteraje in my language. If it proves too difficult for you to use, perhaps you can suggest another."

"I think I can manage that."

"My ... compatriot—?" The words came out as a question.

"That will do fine."

"My compatriot is Jezerix."

The second alien inclined its head.

"I am the leader of this expedition," Xteraje continued. "Jezerix is my mate—a healer and archivist."

"Pleased to meet you both." I stuck out an automatic hand, following the Earthly protocol of manners my mother had battered into my brain as a child. My back spasmed in protest at the sudden movement, and I gasped, biting my lip against the pain.

Jezerix spoke for the first time, with a voice as deep and powerful as James Earl Jones. I revised my mental pictures of them both. "You pain? I help."

I shook my head with a grimace. "Many have tried. None have succeeded."

"They no Vixksinje." (You can see why I call them Visarons.

. . and, I guess, so does everybody else now.)

He unfastened his safety harness and fell to the floor, landing on his feet with an effortless grace. His head came to my waist, but it was obvious he was no child. Muscles rippled under his flight suit, and I cringed back. He proved more than a little intimidating this close.

A grin creased his face. "I no eat you. Too stringy." He made the universal "give it here" gesture toward my hand, and—despite my reservations—I placed it in his.

Almost instantly, a warmth flooded my body. The last jolts of the back spasm were still present, but he concealed them with well-being. He twisted my wrist through a complex series of maneuvers, and when he finished, the pain was gone.

"T-thanks," I mumbled. Though I knew it would be brief, I felt painless for now. My childhood car accident at ten was the last time I had felt pain free. This alien had done in seconds what no doctor had done in forty years.

Xteraje released her own harness and came to stand beside her mate. "Ship repair will take time. Do you have a place to rest?"

"Of course!" I said, giving myself a mental face-palm. "You must be tired. Of course, you are tired. My house lies just across that field." I gestured to the lights of the house shining in the distance. "You are welcome to stay with me as long as you like." I must have been crazy to make such a grand gesture, but in my defense, I was a little high on endorphins at the time.

I led the way home through the dark woods. If I had been superstitious, I would have taken it for a warning of things to come, but I just concentrated on where I put my feet, idly twirling my cane as we went. I didn't need it anymore. It felt glorious.

When we got to the back door of the house, I realized I had no provisions for company. Hell, I usually only saw one or two people a month, and those most often in doctors' offices. What did the Visarons even eat? I should make a quick trip to the store before it closed.

"I need to go down to the store and get some food," I told my impromptu guests. "What would you like?"

Xteraje gave Jezerix a long, meaningful look, and I knew they must be speaking telepathically. When she finally broke the connection, she turned to me. "Whatever you think best. All the food in this world can nourish us. We need no special considerations. Bring what you like."

"*Carte blanche*, huh?" I grinned. Normal trips to the grocery store left me in agony. I hadn't shopped for the fun of it my entire adult life. Surely, this was worth a splurge? "I'll be back as soon as I can."

Stepping into the living room, I turned on the television. "Here, you can watch this until I get back. Maybe it will help with your English."

Without another thought, I grabbed my wallet and keys and headed out the door at 8:45 on a Friday night. Perhaps my more astute readers can guess where this is going.

Despite fifty years of science fiction, fantasy, and horror indoctrination, I did not.

I took my time at the grocery store, buying everything that caught my fancy. Soda, potato chips, three flavors of ice cream, steak, a six-pack of cider—you get the drift. It came to more than a week's paycheck, but it felt good. I felt worth it for once.

Arms full of bags and bottles, I stepped into the kitchen and froze. I stumbled to the table and dropped everything. My heart pounded in my ears at the sound of the television.

"Fifty people killed in a mass shooting today at a retirement party in Illinois. Police are currently blaming it on a disgruntled employee. More details as they come in.

"In other news, a bus collided with a passenger train in California today. Bystanders say the driver paused, then gunned it into the side of the train. No word on casualties as yet.

"And finally, this just in—authorities link a bridge collapse in Wisconsin to faulty engineering practices. Seventeen people died in that tragic incident.

"That is all the news for tonight. Join us tomorrow for updates and information."

Forgetting about ice cream needing a freezer, and everything else I had been so eager to share when shopping, I slipped into the living room.

Xteraje and Jezerix sat side-by-side on the love seat. They might have been life-size dolls for all the animation on their faces.

Xteraje turned to me at last. The ice in her voice terrified me as she spoke. "We came to your world in peace. Looking for a new home, where we could share our knowledge and live as one."

"You can still do that," I whispered. "When people see what Jezerix can do to help people—"

"I don't think so," she replied. "That ship has sailed—as one of your colorful speakers said in one of the non-informational programs we have seen. No, I believe my superiors will revise their expectations now. We will take this planet for our own and use its citizens as they use themselves—to kill for pleasure and hurt for sport. Thank you for sharing the truth with us. When your leaders stand before ours, with our weapons at their throats, we will not fail to tell them we learned it from *YOU*."

PETER KEY

Honorable Mention for Lit Shark's July-August 2024 Poem of the Month

ROCK

Have you ever driven for two hours
to a birthday party, arrived hot and sticky
after getting lost three times, realise
you'd left the gift you'd so painstakingly
shopped for on the sideboard back home,
know no-one but the birthday boy
and his wife, except you find out later
they're no longer together, watch a friend
you'd been looking forward to meeting again
get drunker and drunker, whilst nobody else
says a word to stop him,

Have you?

Have you ever noticed how white walls
are in a doctors' waiting room, how they project
apathy, blankness, conceal all words on diagnosis,
for all kinds of illnesses, don't speak of organ failure,
swelling ankles, weight loss, yellowing of the eyes,
vomiting of blood, confusion, drowsiness, nausea,
liver cirrhosis, how the windows are hidden
to keep the optimism of sunlight at bay.

Well, have you?

Have you ever been at a hospital bedside,
held a hand no longer able to grip,
remember games you played,
pranks you shared, gigs enjoyed, those places

you talked about, but never went,
unspoken words, months without contact.
You watch the saline run dry, listen
to his shallow breathing, count the seconds
in between, wonder why you're the only
one here, why the nurse doesn't reappear,
why you always call him Rock

ANNETTE GAGLIARDI

MY WORDS SLIP

from my lips, down the cleft
of my chin, to hide
beneath my left breast
like shy children.
They grow thin and dissipate
in the night air.

They become ivy, climb
and encircle the old Oak like
a necklace.

My words are stained
and strained with the news
of the day: the murder, mayhem
degradation; the immoral, corrupt,
destitution.

I wail to no avail; cry and sigh—
my words whimper as they drift
like flightless birds on a sightless
journey.

They fall as rain -
Ing leaves in autumn,
running down the days
in ways beyond my comprehension.

CAROL EDWARDS

SURFACE TENSION

Symmetry: opposite identicals, proportional, balanced, even
    aesthetic, pleasing
Water: fluid, flowing
      finding the easiest lanes
         its true shape never seen
           always the form of its vessel, even gravity.

she
    hovers
        cradles

           is cradled in
      the cupped hands
        bone
        stone
      (leaking through and into and under)
  too slow to lift and drink
      satiate the insatiable.

she asks to be passive
      settled,
            she frames the face
  facing the sky facing the mirror facing the moon

      – eternity –

    she cannot hold the body of space
      she cannot open her mouth to drink it
the deepness of her disproportionate

    to the deepness that exists.

        she falls in reflective splendor
           her shape held in perfect tension
                    in perfect   attraction
                          (microscopic chains)
      her symmetry broken with a touch
                        a drop
shards of glass
    the sun splinters to vapor.

DAVID DEPHY

ODE TO LONELINESS

Past cached its calm
in our memory when we

caught that instant
all the shadows

had evaporated
in the cool afternoon.

We shall never see
the hopeless penumbra

of our glances, even
as those past next instant follows,

but can you see,
there is virtually no sound,

just a receding distant noise,
a single wave pulsing

at its very end. Alone here,
steeped in disquieting thoughts

trying to burst into song,
fumbling to utter a single word,

any word. Still, these lips touch the air
and this body is a foreign language

addressing a foreign world.
I say, dig deep, my love,

let us embrace this great void
as an old friend, perhaps then

we shall discover each other
far on the other side of alone.

DALE E. COTTINGHAM

THREE PART POEM

1.

Freedom deceived me. All that talk
that I could be anything I want, say
what I want, live where I want,
say what's on my mind,
as the wind blew, seasons changed,
I thought this life was all about me.
But looking around, others have needs
Make theirselves known.
It turned out not to be so.

Having emerged from school, the day
opens, it is neither blah or bland, I
take a job as the avenues open,
I perform tasks that I make mine,
the days are sufficient, they are either
blue or cloudy. My needs are palpable.
The day is lovely with its own intelligence.
Shadows, grass in wind, isolate house.
Need is what you know, it comes from inside.
No one says yes or no.
I get to know them really well.

2.

You told me come in from the porch
but don't hurry if you aren't done.
I like it on the porch alone with my thoughts.
They rummage over the lowlands,
they can roam without barrier,
take turns, be frisky.

The sun peaks through the haze
revealing grasslands, a few trees,
things building to today's torque.
So many things I could do today.
Weeds reaching into blue sky:
Aren't I still me with others?
Aren't I still me alone?

3.

There is the possibility of change
everywhere, the way the low clouds course on wind.
This part consists of signs
that we could ignore: cars rusting
in fields, oilfield machinery stacked.
The low hills take all thin in, allow.
Promise rises like prayers out kitchen windows.

My vision get keen:
I went to bed last night
and had a dream, not about you this time.
I was sitting in a room at a table.
There were others there
but not paying attention as a woman straddled me,
as if I'd become lovely.

Native grass rises beyond the road.
It is a season smaller because of what we did before,
or what we failed to do.
We could sleep together again tonight
but it will only be a backdrop
to this burning I feel,
all those luscious words and moaning wind
as if a storms come up,
I burn but am not consumed.

S. ABDULWASI'H OLAITAN

Honorable Mention for Lit Shark's March-April 2024 Poem of the Month

SILENT SOLILOQUY: CONTEMPLATION OF REDISCOVERY & GRIEVANCE.

every time   i trace the lines of grievance / this country install in me / on a paper of intersection / i question my citizenship & the patchwork of my language in a land that doesn't claim me as its soil / mother invents a new software of grievance to the ocean floor of my tristesse /   that not all poems should be metaphor-ized / metaphor is for children who / gently / play harp / creating ballads for the snowman /   forgetting it only lasts a winter / not grief / for grief itself is poetry/ poetry? an elegy of how we become a baby child / in the face of anything visible / that dissolves / past the sun / past the moon / past the light in the sight of darkness /   casting a long shadow across the lawn / maami says; every mouth is but a liar of sincerity /for a piece of meat declared wanted in a pallor of throat / is but every mouth talent / of all the places i have known   / as pagoda of cacoethes & cravings / this woolgathering with its unremarkable walls / & foreign fences / is a weirdest room to call home / this is the crossfire / my faces all over a wreckage of forsaken path / lured into letting go of everything i own that was never mine / seduced by the cadaver of a dream yet / i rediscovered myself again in this poem / yet, i rediscovered my reflection again in this wide hungry den   / that to(day) /   i become a guinea fowl / guinea fowl? after escaping the egg / guinea fowl follows the first one he sees at / all cost/

JANINA AZA KARPINSKA

BEACHED

We walk under an oil-slick sky in gabardine macs,
shouldering a headwind like seasoned rugby players,
inching along lines of exhausted seaweed
searching for treasure.

I find a whip of a fish—a stiff cord of muscle
the colour of unbleached linen. He finds
a teaspoon from Virgin Atlantic—embedded in sand.

I marvel at the marbled skin of a headless dogfish,
which, he tells me, is a kind of shark. I run
a finger—tail-ward along firm flesh, but in
trying to reverse the move, I'm gripped by tiny cells,
astonished at such a feat of paralysis. Is it like
that between us? Is there no going back?

And then we stumble across the unlikely fruit
of a coconut; a footnote from Paradise, perhaps.

CHRIS WOOD

TALE OF THE TWIN RED OAKS

Forgotten acorns, buried by fox squirrels,
sprout the day Wall Street crashed.
As the stock market plummeted,
tender leaves reached for the sun.

They grew through the sadness—
the Great Depression, the Dust Bowl,
war. Bud in the days of rock 'n' roll,
poodle skirts, and Elvis. Blossom
with lava lamps and bell bottoms
as man landed on the moon. Roots deepen
while Pac-Man gobbles the arcade
and the Berlin Wall crashes to the ground.
Thrive through the Clinton years,
then knuckle and gnarl in the new millennia.

A home to ravens' nests and owl dens
hollowed out by woodpeckers,
they still stand tall, surviving progress,
at the edge of the parking lot
outside my office window. Their leaves,
a brilliant crimson, flame the horizon
this November morning, falling
like lit matches to the wet ground.

DALE E. COTTINGHAM

TO MY FATHER FROM A NEW CLIMATE

Somewhere you still wear your work shoes, pants,
your shirt still oil-stained, the same slight shoulders
you used to lever transmissions out of cars,
your hazel eyes allowing the world in,
this world that would seem somehow familiar
but strange: oceans rising, refugees in boats,
the climate having collected our debris,
offering a critique all its own.

Our nightly congress at the dinner table,
how you led off, gave us admonitions, tips,
but allowed us to have our say,
providing us with civil options
for the uncivil times to come.

World I take part in,
can't look away from,
even if I wanted to.

You knew I was weak all along.

I miss you, wish we had a few minutes
to talk not man to man, but human
to human, words coming easy as breathing,
so I could ask you if your faith served you still.
You've known me all my life, till suddenly,
you weren't there, and I had to carry on.

I remember clasping your finger
as we crossed the church parking lot,

finger bigger than mine now,
finger intimate with transmissions,
finger knowledgeable of women,
the world, the climate of your time.

I couldn't know then what you knew then,
just as you can't know
what I know now, small and large,
all absorbed into the climate, all,
as you would say, just part of it.

S. ABDULWASI'H OLAITAN

WHAT SPOILED THIS POEM IS THE ALARM OF LOSS

this is how every prayer starts: "Ya Allah!" my village's devout men would say "O' father" making their hands the confluence of supplications _connecting each drop of tears to heaven. their voices rising like hymns at break of day, i see their prayers sprouting like flowers in the orchard of heart rooted deep in faith, they marry their watery eyelids to the liners in their palms but my mother forgets these formalities. instead, her tears are saddle with bridges of that public song, her suffering from losing her stamen to the rain is almost three times as great as a day's misery. while sitting on her knees, she is searching for words. words that best capture a broken plea poised to burst from her quivering lips. father was on his cushion. no, on his bed. no, in the backyard. yes, __finding a perfect place in the vast expanse of the sky to bury his curious tears but he couldn't help it. he couldn't hide behind the proverb; 'be a man' as nature's beauty moves his inner testament to weep. tears broke upon his gazing at a star falling off the portrait of a single-mother sky. mother changes her position. she lets her tears flow from her prayer. yusuf is at the front gate of heaven where prayer is better off commissions: one leg walks on earth & one leg in the sky. mother keeps on chewing words like promise, in spite of the agony of loss in her voice. maybe those prayers may gather a moss and name him 'ko ku man' meaning; "forever resides." God is up sitting on his throne, my mother is on her velvet prayer-rug seeking solace in the reign of night, i was looking at my brother's soul, lying downwards on the ground flat: broken & shredded, disoriented in the shadows. his hands are cold, my fears are colder. i fail to consume my fears before they sprout and devour me. i see some stanzas of poetry dying in his feet, he was like a weak cicada larva that can not even squirm. then, i join my mother in heart &   sing along with her,   i turn my tongue into prayers;

> // "ya rabb, i seek refuge in you from the pedals
> that carry my music here. is there still some healthy irish smiles
> returning to my brother's face? see. see the grace on his skin
> migrating from its callant, please, 'Ya rabb' resuscitate him.
> although my prayers are smaller than
> a soy sauce plate compared to my mom's
> who has lived heavens many times in your feet
> just to see your eyes, at least
> we are making our way in the familiar general trajectory."

in silence, i whispered my prayers low but before i could say all of them, the candle flickered, then broke within his absence. the joints of hope are dislocated. now, tell me, how can the eyes of a little young boy ever be at rest? my muscles are covered by the rhythm of loss, i turn my spit into prayers, even if they're not going to revive him_at least they can walk him home in my stead.

DIANA WOODCOCK

STOKING HOPE'S LAST EMBER

    Escape all the bad news of late,
       enter a temperate rainforest,
  the Great Smokies with its nearly three
       thousand miles of streams and
  rivers through which one can catch
       wisps of neon orange and lemon yellow,

  purples and pinks till one thinks
       s/he might be hallucinating—
  so illuminating is the show happening
       under the flow of a mountain stream
  early summer. Mating season for
       Tennessee, Warpaint and Saffron shiners,

  for Central stonerollers swarming and
       spawning above pebbled mounds—
  waterfall sounds all around. The mystery
       of birth, growth, death revealed in every
  river and stream in these blue-veiled
       mountains with their ferns and trilliums,

  mosses and old-growth trees. Everything
       pungent and damp, make camp
  beside a waterfall far from disaster
       and affliction, and realize it is all
  you need to feed the hunger and stoke
       the last ember of hope.

FIVE:
THE CRIME OF EXISTING

ABIGAIL OTTLEY

TURNING TURTLE

I've been wearing it so long I forget it's there. You could say over time it's grown into me. I'm like one of those turtles you see on social media with lengths of fishing twine or fine, silver wire embedded in the flesh of their necks. Except I have no rescuer. No one has hauled me from the water, notwithstanding my thrashing and snapping. No one has snipped with infinite patience at the tightness that cuts off my breath. Nor has anyone caressed me as they bathed the open wound, cleansing it of pus and infection. No one whispered soft words to ease my great sadness before giving me back to the deep. In my own case, there can be nothing like that. The gag was tied tight. I accepted it. Soon I grew used to it, then I learned to love it. That's a very hard thing to admit. The truth is when you're young, bad things can be done to you, things that frighten and hurt you and, unless you are lucky and someone hauls you up, you will likely take the blame upon yourself. Now I am older. I see how these things work. I might wish I had been lucky, like those turtles. I wasn't lucky. I lived in a world where children and turtles don't count.

ROY ADAMS

LOST

Beyond the fire lurking low
the cub close by to where we stood
went unseen but in her wake
our bin was bare; next day though
moving easy through the woods
she took steps a mutt might take.

Then upright swaying—to, fro
she seemed to say "where's the goods?"
As if pals at hearty play
we gaped at her graceful show
big-eyed, wide grins stretching broad
when it dawned: this was no game.

We gathered handy stones to
hustle her into the woods
then mom appeared at the brake.
Our ruse at first made them go
but not for long, we understood.
We packed, stroked across the lake.

At our new site by fire's glow,
guide's tale froze our festive mood.
Destiny had raised the stakes:
their new mien a dead-end slough—
ease with man and untamed blood,
for them and us, baneful freight.

D.C. BUSCHMANN

POEM ON A FEW LINES OF BILLY COLLINS'S WHALE DAY

Every night when I lie down,
I turn my back on half the world
to block out visions of
human stalkers and their prey.
Meanwhile, thousands of whales are cruising
along at various speeds under the seas.
I hope they hold their breaths on the cold ocean floor
long enough to escape windmills or whalers,
who harvest their oil, their bones, their teeth,
their very souls from their lifeless bodies.
Also, elephants.
Humans still trophy hunt these massive,
intelligent, social creatures, who
travel in herds, nurse their young, form
life-long attachments, bury their dead
and grieve like humans.
And for what?
To have pictures framed to display
in their homes. Smiling beside "their kill."
Proud of snuffing out innocent breath,
a creature merely living its life—caring for calves,
the elderly and ailing, moseying toward
the water hole, eating wild ginger leaves,
bark, coconut seedlings, roots and fruits—proud
to have disrupted a family unit, a herd,
to have ended a gentle life.

DIANA WOODCOCK

MUD DEVIL OR ANGEL?

Try feeling tender
toward the hellbender—
a slimy salamander known as mud
devil, snot otter, lasagna lizard,
Allegheny alligator in decline
due to water pollution, habitat loss,
modification of their stream homes—

the solution: to protect acres of forest
land across the Appalachian region,
not as hard as it seems—we just need to
restore streams, revitalize forests,
realize how urgent is the task to safe-
guard nature's intricate web of life.

Maintainers of the river's ecology
and crayfish populations, they are indicators
of high-quality water, habitat alteration,
environmental change—registering
the impact sooner than most species.
Living quiet lives tucked away under

large rocks in mountain streams
Arkansas to New York, they're so
often mistaken for a rock.
Considering the fat snot otter,
try practicing self-forgetfulness,
returning to a frame of mind—that time

of childlikeness—full of questions and
curiosity: How did it come to be?
How many still exist? Be transfixed
by it. The closer you get, the sharper
she pierces your heart till you become
one with her—with her struggle to exist,

to persist in polluted waters, in shrinking
habitat. Just like that, she becomes
your sister, and you feel deeply for her
as she shimmies across your path, and just
like that, you awaken out of depression
and self-obsession. She makes a gap,

a crack through which the light pours—
her subtle magical appearance
just what your aching heart needs
here and now after so much loss.
Feeling tender toward the hellbender,
you become a woman unburdened

by the world's and her own tribulations,
and you turn to celebration of the numinous—
of the whole universe as home—and one
mud devil your personal angel distracting you
from all the ignoble and cruel man-made
disasters of these dark times.

One hellbender filling you with love
and wonder and evidence
heaven can be (is) this very instance
                underfoot.

MARK STROHSCHEIN

SANCTUARY OF VOICES

—for Wolfie

each step on sand & sliding scree
accepting us into its crunchy-foot fold

random rocks tumble from bluff's bulge
like ghosts tapping shoulders

reminding us to stay alert, to evince
how nature burdens us with erosion

rivulet-making water of unknown source
trickles mystifyingly from high above

perhaps it all began when they built
that Temple of Seaweed

stuck those four wooden posts in the sand
and kelp-danced around in their joy-collecting

searching shoreline, scraping, upturning rocks
amidst *whooshing* of weary waves & sandpiper cries

praying for Turkish towel & witch's hair
for winged kelp, wakame & studded sea balloon

for sugar kelp, kombu & sargassum
for blackweed, bladderwrack & nori

for green of tuft, lettuce & rope
for feather boa, dulse & dead man's fingers

for bleach weed, bull & bullwhip kelp
for soda straws & split kelp

hanging their fragile adhesive remains
on their wooden altar to dry, harvest & honor

the fire forged: rivulets ran
rocks rumbled from recesses

and the wind-sculpted face of talus slope
sang its slippery song of descent

vowing never
to be silenced

CHRISTA FAIRBROTHER

PAIN IS A SHARK

Pain casts you out to sea where the predators wait, spinning fins and shadows. Sleep apnea circles, just as you're nodding off, it draws close, a bump to make sure you're still paying attention. Then back to cat and mouse. Pain's just waiting, wearing you down. The sun, the salt, the struggle, they'll do the job. Patient, it knows one night you'll slide off your makeshift raft into its rows, rows of erupting teeth.

how did you come to
be a castaway, was the
storm worse than the wreck

BETH KANELL

CICADAS HATCHING

What would be the point of sleeping a hundred years
if nothing changed—the lips of the prince sticky and warm
and the ring of trees around the castle thorned and thick?

Cicadas savor a cleansing fast from romance and hot lust
serene in their darkness, tymbals still, no click or clatter, no song
then after seventeen orbits of the sun they stir

wake into a miracle of difference. Out of solitude and silence
into the winged wonder of a thousand thousand golden bodies—
chorus of desire, music lifting. This lure of longing.

This honey-hearted multitude. Scraping outward, shivering,
with reddened eyes they scan the kingdom. Potent, proofed, they
     climb,
summon spouses, tymbals trembling, fierce and fertile.

Who among humans holds a president's seat as long? Or keeps
a crown steady, a belt of office cinched and sufficient? Pride
may pose a stumbling block for sultans and sophisticates

but not to cicadas: Pride is their purred and pure response
to perfect certainty. Only cicadas, through unblinking scarlet eyes,
catch starlight on each set of transparent wings

and inject it into trees with their promise: "We shall return.
We are the measure of your fairy-tale frail forever."

CHRIS WOOD

EARTHING

Mint deters beetles and mosquitoes.
I crush the leaves in my palms,
rub them on my arms and legs,
as I watch ants sashay across the brick
ledge by the front stoop,
and listen to warblers and wrens
drown out the lawnmower down the street.

I walk barefoot, ground my soul
with each step, breathe in the aroma
of the freshly cut grass, reconnect with nature
as the green releases tension from my shoulders.
Crickets switch daylight to dark
and fireflies light remnants of my thoughts
as the stings of today subsides.

AMBER SAYER

MALIGNED MOTHER

The streamlined ladies are feared sea predators, horror movies made about their kind, their teeth hung on souvenir necklaces like prize game hanging on a hunter's wall.

But the scaly maidens aren't just a dorsal-finned ferocious ocean beast haunting the blue void; they are cartilaginous acrobats as diverse and misunderstood as the deep waters they travel.

The future carpetshark mother will lay her eggs in a leathery pouch borne from her own body. She will swim for hours trying to find the safest nursery among the reefs to leave her precious mermaid purse. She reluctantly swims away from the leathery pocket housing secrets, trying to take solace in the fact that she's sealed it with everything the tiny pearls will need before they hatch as swimmers and join the seas.

Others, like the hammerhead, masquerade as a mammalian mother, her body becoming increasingly less sleek as her young mature inside her womb. She may be a burdened seafarer for up to three years with the same pup stretching the boundaries of her uterus, eventually releasing her full-grown toothy baby into the inky sea.

Some, like the great white lady, will perform exquisite underwater choreography with a masculine dance partner. Then, she endures the painful stabs of his chiseled hooks and claspers piercing her fins for a brief impregnation. She will groan in the haze of her own blood leaching into the coldness he's left her with, as his dorsal fin being swallowed by the dark abyss will be the last time she'll ever see him. But her body is a specimen of the marvels of Darwin's contributions, her skin three times thicker than his and a quick-healing cloak of armor.

Other finned females will embark on long oceanic

journeys after mating, ensuring their young are raised in just the right waters. Each of these mothers is a fickle house hunter, looking for a warm estuary or seamount so that her babies emerge into friendly seas but she is worried; the same species that makes films about her own kinds' attacks are destroying the best nursery habitats for her young.

No matter how she brings her pups into the aqueous world, each shark mother will meet the same fate: swimming the waters alone. Her young will fight the seas themselves, not maturing to the stage to engage in the labors she's endured for many years. She hopes that by that time, her child will swim in seas where she is recognized as much for her unique natural beauty, vital role in protecting biodiversity in her apex predator post, and the 4000 years of evolutionary wonder her family has survived, as she is seen as a paradigm of danger or killed for her powerful fins. As she plunges towards the sea floor, she finds herself realizing that the one species that seems to fear her the most is the very same one that she herself fears.

DIANA WOODCOCK

ELEGY FOR ONE THOUSAND-PLUS MANATEES

How could we have let it happen—
let them starve as their seagrass meadows
were poisoned,* their habitats
desecrated? Albert** was right—
[man] will end by destroying the earth
because *he's lost the capacity to foresee
and forestall.* How many dead
manatees does it take to wake
us up? You'd think after 500,
even just 125 in 2021, we would have
opened our eyes—would have realized.
Finally, after more than a thousand,
something is done.

The Lunar New Year's new moon,
thread-thin, shines down on this
Arabian lagoon where cousins of
Florida's manatees—dugongs—
also exist at risk, their struggle a
poignant reflection of the moment—
so much loss, so many vanishing
landscapes. The heart breaks
as one observes how dugongs and
manatees move along quietly,
gravely, grey as an overcast day,
like a psalm, a lament, their sea-
grasses burning, turning into poison.

They are gentle, made of blood and
bones, day after day cruising their
watery grassy meadows in search of
sustenance, not crying out or com-
plaining—at least not in words we
comprehend. They are as patient,
long-suffering as saints. And when they
go marching/swimming in, man will
not be *in that number*.

    *   Manatees rely mainly on sea grass, beds of which have been smothered by pollutants along with outbreaks of toxic algae blooms intensified by climate change.

   **   "Albert" as in Albert Schweitzer—known as a musician, theologian, physician, and a true humanitarian.

BETH MARQUEZ

INFIDELITY

Crocodiles don't
die. Their hunger grows as they
age. Until they starve.

JULIAN MATTHEWS

THE LAST BEE

At sunrise, in our garden, the shrubbery is speckled with
    bejeweled dew,
flowers like hungry beaks open to greet mother sun and
    I'm pottering about
with a trowel, when the sounds of a bee buzzing in and out
    of the wild pink
and purple hyacinths, growing at the untrimmed hedge, catches my
    post-coffee attention.

Mr Google says a single bee produces one 12th of a teaspoon of honey
in its entire short lifetime. That's a dozen hardworking fellas
    which sacrificed
their lives for a single teaspoon that went into my cereal this morning.
A New Scientist story says the average honeybee lives only 18 days
these days, down from 34 days, almost a 50% fall over the past
    five decades.
Another article speculates how bees may go extinct by 2050.

I see the bee before me has not read the science, nor does she care.
Busy is as busy does. Tiny pollen sticks to her head, torso, legs
like waxy beads as she flits away. She'll visit an average of a thousand
flowers today alone, pollinating thousands more in those last days
    of her life—

I go over your excuses now, your rebuffs, your last replies: "I'm busy!"
went the usual refrain, or "Maybe, next week," until all the maybes
    evaporated
into the ether, the messaging stopped, and the screen went dark
    forever.

I reminisce in this beautiful garden we grew, with the heat rising,
the bees now disappearing from view, these emptied flowers, and
    everything
I remember of you, all the foraged memories falling off leaves like
    the last drips
of dew, as I turn towards our living hive, its dead queen,
and the sting of another ugly cry.

DUSTIN BROWN

THE LAST JELLYFISH

The last jellyfish died last night,
harpooned by a philanthropist
off the shallow coast of Madeira.
The biologists harbored their burets,
the politicians blamed each other.

I will miss their swarms,
when they surrounded me at twilight
with weightless, interlaced tentacles
in glittering magenta clouds
that saved me, for a moment, from drowning.

ZENIA DEHAVEN

THE CRIME OF EXISTING

On June 7th, 2024, three swimmers were injured by sharks on Walton Beach, a Florida beach bordering the Gulf of Mexico. A 45-year-old woman lost the lower half of her arm and was hospitalized in critical condition. Two young girls, ages 15 and 17, were waist-deep in water when they were attacked. One sustained minor injuries and the other was hospitalized.

Shortly after the news of these attacks broke, I was scrolling on TikTok and came across a video of someone filming the beach where the attacks took place. The person filming stood on a balcony overlooking the coast. They zoomed in on a long, dark silhouette slinking through the shallow water, gasping as a black dorsal fin cut through the aquamarine surface. The video alleged that this was the finned attacker swimming away from the crime scene.

I hope all three victims recover quickly. But, as I encountered more and more news coverage and social media blips spreading the word of dangerous beaches and unpredictable shark behavior, I couldn't help but wonder why we scorn animals for the crime of being animals.

Contrary to the movie *Jaws*, which unfairly portrayed sharks as villainous, bloodthirsty monsters, sharks are not malicious. No evidence supports the idea that sharks stalk human-infested beaches in hopes of snacking on an unsuspecting vacationer. There are several theories explaining why sharks bite humans. One theory suggests that sharks use biting to explore their environment. They don't have hands or limbs, and thus their mouths are their primary way to investigate the unknown. Shark attacks may also occur because of mistaken identity. They may interpret the shadow of a swimming surfer as a seal. This could be why many shark bites on people are shallow. In these instances, the shark bit a human and realized it wasn't a fish, seal, or other marine animal listed on its usual dinner menu, and swam off.

Despite these attacks on June 7th, shark attacks are rare. In 2023, there were about 70 shark attacks worldwide, with only 10 of these attacks proving fatal (International Shark Attack File). In comparison, elephants were the cause of over 500 human fatalities in 2022 (Statista), yet elephants remain a beloved animal by our standards. We have the stuffed plushies to prove it. Why are elephants revered as wise and regal while sharks are viewed as predatory and dangerous?

While these statistics support that sharks are not aggressive and attacks on humans are scarce, it's ridiculous that we must defend their existence. Why do we criticize sharks for being wild animals? Why are we angry at them when we are the ones stepping into their home turf? Where are they supposed to go?

I've swam in open water for as long as I can remember. I love the ocean. I love when the waves sweep me onto shore, laughing and spitting up salt water. I love floating above small schools of fish, careful not to move or blow bubbles so I don't disturb them. But I know the ocean is not my home, even though I attempted to learn how to breathe underwater as a kid. Even then, though, I knew to be respectful of the remarkable creatures that call the rolling waters home. I didn't even like all of the animals that roamed beneath the surface, particularly spiny sea urchins and drifting jellyfish, but I knew it was unfair of me to loathe them when I was the one entering their home. Now, if jellyfish sprouted legs and appeared at my doorstep, all bets are off.

We are afraid of animals that have a threatening reputation, like sharks (*Jaws* did a number on the general public), even if that reputation is misconstrued or entirely false. Many fear bees for their capacity to sting. While some have a severe allergy to their venom, in which case their apprehensive approach to bees is understandable, there is still a surplus of people who don't have a life-threatening allergy to bees who are terrified of them. Bees don't fly around humans searching for a victim. They may be attracted to certain people based on their smell; they love the smell of particular shampoos, sunscreens, and perfumes. They're also drawn to flowery prints and shiny accessories like watches and jewelry. They hover around people because they're curious, not because they're looking for an exposed patch of skin to sting. Bees sting when they're threatened, such as if a human harasses their hive or swats at them.

I have a firsthand experience of bees' reluctance to sting. When I was in elementary school, I rode horses. I wore boot-cut pants to make it easier to slip my boots on and off. One day, a bee managed to fly up the rim of my pant leg and buzzed against my calf, trapped. I panicked, dismounting my steed, and sprinted into the equipment shed, locking the door behind me. I sat down and guided the black-and-yellow intruder out, careful not to prod or poke at it in the process. It buzzed lazy circles around my head before flying away.

As absurd as the tale sounds, it's true. To this day, I have yet to be stung by a bee. According to an analysis by the Harvard School of Public Health, the chances of being stung by a bee is about six million to one.

Finally, humans harbor ill sentiment towards scavenging animals because of their association with death even though these creatures are crucial to preventing the spread of disease. Bottom feeders, which are aquatic animals that feed on or near the bottom of a body of water, including loaches and catfish, sometimes specialize in scavenging bodies killed by other predators. And yet, even though these animals help reduce the amount of decay and harmful chemicals in the water, we use the term "bottom feeder" as an insult to describe someone who has low status or value in society.

Vultures are particularly stigmatized for their role as scavengers. Like all scavengers, they feed on the bodies of dead animals, but, because of their unattractive, bald heads and their habit of circling dead or dying animals, we view them as repulsive. We often see them on the side of a road, picking the meat off road-kill and hopping out of the way when cars journey too close. This makes us associate them with death and gore. The word "vulture" itself is used to describe somebody who tries to take advantage of someone else who is in a bad situation. Our disgust of them is completely unjustifiable given how crucial they are to balancing our ecosystem. Vultures rapidly consume carrion before it decays, and their stomachs contain an acid that destroys many of the harmful substances found in dead animals (National Geographic). If vultures were to go extinct, carcasses would remain exposed to the environment for weeks, resulting in the build-up of harmful diseases and bacteria, such as anthrax and rabies, which harms both wildlife and humans (Wildlife ACT). Vultures may not be the most attractive birds, but they're so crucial to our ecosystem that we should embrace them, even if they are a bit ugly.

Unfortunately, it is not enough to acknowledge that these species are unjustly stigmatized. All three of these animals are suffering at the hands of humans.

One shocking study suggests that human activities kill between 100 million sharks a year (Science). The researchers reviewed fisheries data from 150 countries and interviewed experts on the subject, including scientists, environmental advocates, and fisheries workers. Overfishing is a huge threat to sharks, which are targeted for their fins or accidentally killed when they're caught alongside other fish. It's estimated that about 50 million sharks are killed as by catch each year (Animal Welfare Institute). Legislation designed to prevent shark finning (in which the shark fins are cut from the body and the rest of the shark is thrown into the ocean to die) may have hurt sharks in the long run. Now, fishers are encouraged to keep the whole shark. The anti-finning legislation might have accidentally incentivized a new market for shark meat. To put this gruesome information into perspective, for every person who is attacked by a shark annually, over 1.4 million sharks die.

While they may be a nuisance at a picnic, bees are one of the most important animals on the planet. A third of the world's food production depends on bees (UN Environment Programme). Bees and other pollinators, including butterflies, bats, and hummingbirds, are increasingly threatened by human development. Bee populations are declining due to habitat loss, intensive farming practices, and the excessive use of agrochemicals such as pesticides. Iowa, for instance, has lost more than 99% of its tall-grass prairie because of agriculture (Vox). Prairies are home to wildflowers and are a very important landscape for bees. While honey bees aren't endangered, many native bees are at risk of dying out. More than a quarter of North American bumblebees are threatened by extinction (Vox). So, next time there's a bee buzzing annoyingly close to you, reconsider before succumbing to frustration and swatting it away.

Even vultures aren't spared from the onslaught of human activity. Like sharks and bees, vultures suffer as humans expand their communities and agricultural lands. Infrastructure like power lines pose dangers for the large birds during flight. Agricultural expansion forces vultures out of their territory and reduces the amount of carrion they can scavenge. On top of that, vultures are threatened by poachers. Because vultures flock to animal carcasses, they potentially give away the location of poachers' illegal activities. To remain undetected, poachers poison animal carcasses to kill vultures. In Africa, breeding pairs of vultures have declined by 70% because of poachers (National Geographic). Of the 23 living species of vultures, over half of them are considered Threatened, Endangered, or Critically Endangered as a result of humans (Discover Wildlife).

This may sound grim and dire, largely because it is grim and dire, but there are ways that we as everyday humans can help. There are a multitude of organizations dedicated to the conservation of these precious animals. I've listed a few of them below. It isn't an exhaustive list, but it's a good place to get started if you want to help these incredible creatures and stay informed.

Shark Conservation Organizations:
    1. Shark Stewards
    2. Saving the Blue
    3. Bimini Shark Lab

Bee Conservation Organizations:
    1. The Bee Conservancy
    2. Xerces Society for Invertebrate Conservation
    3. Save the Bees

Vulture Conservation Organizations:
    1. Vulture Conservation Foundation
    2. Vulture Conservancy
    3. IUCN Vulture Specialist Group

All of this to say, don't judge a shark for his teeth, a bee for her stinger, or a vulture for his diet. Be kind to animals, whether they be predators, pollinators, or scavengers.

    They need our help now more than ever.

SIX: CLIMATE CHANGE

DALE E. COTTINGHAM

WINTER

You are back but changed,
warmer, drier than before.
What happened? I mean,
we used to dress all season in hats, coats,
bundle in the old way,
we thought we knew you.

During the meeting her mind
wandered to what she did last summer,
skinny dipping, and who she did it with,
all that swaying in the lake,
swaying in the lake house,
she was taking her chance.
But morning arrived like truth,
the sun cast a harsher light.

And even if I wanted to go to you,
so we could nest on the lowlands,
savor each breath,
I can't. We've both gone other places,
done other things, leaving me
torn, divided, with the bitter taste of regret.

But you, O winter, debonaire, suave,
have shown us how to change.

URSULA MCCABE

RAIN'S ENSEMBLE

December rain is constant, a stream runs
between my booted feet, rivulets define the path,
round the corner
a dangling cedar limb splashes wet.

It's a dark morning
movie locations replay for my
muddled head; the opening scene about
the logging family
living on an isolated bend of an Oregon river.
In the old movie *Sometimes a Great Notion*.
Henry Fonda grimaces as he takes on the town.

There's Richard Jaeckel's frantic eyes,
he is drowning in the water,
so much rain,
a stuck log holds him down.

Inside home my footsteps know the floor boards
and their sounds.
Soft rabbit feet find themselves
missing a known chair, table corners
shrink. I'm out of the rain
sipping coffee in low light,
the old movie still plays on.

Considering all my sins,
and there are some—
the rain is welcome during this short day—

not one Douglas fir stands between me and
the bed where you sleep with our dog.

My head is above water,
no logjams block my river.
I will join you till dawn trips round.

CHRISTIANA DOUCETTE

THE SEA SERPENT

You've heard the wind howl.
But have you heard it scream?
The storm is a sea snake
coiling around reefs and roofs.
Supplicant palm trees
bend double to the sonic bursts
splinter, splay wide
before the double fanged wave and wind.
Roads, run rivers of poison
between lightning forked tongues.
It crashes up the coastline.

The land shudders
as the ocean gulps
islands and cities,
bays and beaches,
buildings and bodies.
Venom slithers through culverts
hisses through suburbia.
It slips, drips, sips
up streets and sidewalks,
steps and decks,
trailers and cars,
doorways and windows,
walls and rafters,

Squeezing, swallowing,
shredding, shedding swathes of sand,
rolling outward,
uncoiling its engorged carcass
in swollen ripples.

DAVID DEPHY

HEADWINDS

Kissed by the wind
like a sail, the galleon
drives on. I have been
drowned and opened,
made whole and poignant
by a wind who casts me adrift.

Oh wind, I am made
of quenching aspirations.
The passion
of your sea lives
within me,
and that old kiss
quenches me

like a song.

LAUREN K. NIXON

FORCED

encroaching frost is the herald for their sudden shift
their abduction, enslavement
torn from sodden, autumn earth and steel-silver sky
and thrust into the long dark
packed close with horse shit and woollen waste
straining in perpetual night
for their two-year memory of light

they will be long and slender
sanguine and tender
before they're carted to the tracks and sold
pale leaves trembling as they rumble towards the capital
to kitchens, to be pared and sliced
civilised into dishes
fit for a table dressed in white linen

it is said you can hear the rhubarb groaning
when you pass the forcing sheds

DIANA WOODCOCK

WITH WHALE SHARKS

Playing host to more than one hundred
whale sharks off Qatar's north coast,
above the Al Shaheen oil field, the Arabian
Gulf's warm waters provide just
what the threatened species needs.

Late April to October they gather—
even through summer when surface sea
temperatures reach over 35 degrees celsius—
cooler Indian Ocean water drawn in
by high evaporation rates. The mixing

of currents and oil platforms overgrown
with coral turned into artificial reefs
just what a whale shark needs—eggs
from spawning tuna. Watching
the world's largest fish, I wish

those who dump trash and toxic waste
into the seas could see what I see—
the majesty of this one species,
and feel the need to live in harmony
with all creatures. With whale sharks,

I watch the sun rise and set over
an Arabian oasis. The oceans turned now
into garbage dumps, and yet these sharks
off Qatar's coast thriving. I drink a toast
to them, the hope they inspire, what they

say to us by their enduring presence of
sixty million years—wisdom there are no
words for. Disgusted with all the talk
and plans to clean up the mess we've made,
I turn now to the amazing whales—

to their warm saline waters, the sun
above them blazing, the days full of haze.
I would spend them shakened out of
complaceny as I listen to whale sharks
talking among themselves.

Hardened by the world, I am softened
and rescued by these sharks. Filled
with admiration for these ones mired
in the sea's desolation, I pray them well,
       and beg Gaia for a miracle.

LAUREN K. NIXON

STORM PETREL

Its potential infects the water, a cauldron
boiling over rocks, over salt-shingle,
the fore-running wind whips up
spray into meringue, tussling with
bright mounds of thrift and kidney vetch.

A shadow flits, the gaze's thief;
describes an arc, a tangent,
darting between the real and the not-quite.
An abbreviation, fighting the wind.

She is early this year, my elegant friend,
getting in ahead of the rush.
Her fellows will be along soon,
but this nondescript Sunday she races
fishing boats, scrying their passage home.

SEVEN:
BIRDS OF THE AIR

GTIMOTHY GORDON

Winner of Lit Shark's May-June 2024 Poem of the Month

MEADOWLARK, WALT, ME

Meadowlark sunning itself
on new high-end hacienda digs
cupola away from barrel cacti
and cottonwood, solitary, hermetic,
not many here of his kind, desert-savvy,
restless, saluting dawn in clear, sharp notes
until full light, the go-by patter turn achy,
warbly and gushy, dead-on dreamy I know,
and I know he's not just crooning to dawn,
would-be few mates, just to himself,
content with his own song, voice,
I like to think, sounding very much mine,
Walt's, of absent lover, significant other,
life partner, hanging like a lonely corner cowboy
waiting for that girl in the flatbed Ford
trolling Outback edge a second, third, time
for a closer look at him, our old Walt, me.

LAUREN K. NIXON

IT'S SINGLES DAY IN THE 'BURBS

all that feathery finery plumped
starlings do the puff and ruffle
in the queue around the bird feeder,
Better get those nesting boxes ready, Baby

cock robin (the other one) does
a four-toed strut along the trellis
wiggling his bum, *look at me, look*
the sparrows in the bird bath flick

diamantes at the girls they want to impress
though there are a few couples in the crowd
blackbird picking up last year's squeeze
the tits returning to their comfort zones

a wren with a big voice complains
that he cannot get a date
for love nor shepherd's purse
quiets as the gang of magpies,

neighbourhood bullies, make
an entrance, riffing *one for sorrow
two for joy, three for a girl, four for—*
a blur of orange and brown—

the cock robin (the OG) careens into
his rival, knocks him into the bird bath
scattering belligerent sparrows
the crowd lifts, leaving the feeder

swinging, casting disco ball flashes
across the apple tree where a pair
of wood pigeons look on, haughty
and secure in their monogamy

preening dust from each other's
primaries as the sparrows come
back, bellowing songs of lust
a return to the status: crow

MARK STROHSCHEIN

HERON RISES

startled by footsteps
we negotiate new tense space
in minor-miracle moment

under dramatic pastels
sage of swamp & sky
rises like a shoot of

good luck bamboo
greets air with swish of
solemn wing sweep

DOUG VAN HOOSER

SECOND BROOD

For days I watch the two of you. The razor cut red head
flitting branch to branch, couching behind the Korean lilac's

leaves. Watching his auburn tinted partner's hustle and bustle.
A carpenter of leaves, twigs, and a paper scrap. New home for

a second brood. Did she choose the hibiscus for the camouflage?
Thousands of variegated, wing shaped leaves that whisper

a lullaby in the wind? But you never take occupancy. Vanish
like the moon in sunlight, abandon the nest. Was it the scurrying

chipmunks, a thunderstorm's rancor, my looming face staring
out the window? A week later I see her hopping branch to branch

inspecting the abutilon's orange bells. On the other side of the house,
I see his crimson flash dash across the conifers' green screen.

Cardinals do not divorce. Makes me wonder if there's a spat. She
unhappy with her own construct? A second home too much work?

Him singing location, location, location; new doesn't mean better.
Perhaps second thoughts on a second brood? The first round fledged,

dispersed in the woods leaves you searching for a way to fill your day.

URSULA MCCABE

MORNINGS

out canyon way
shadows collide down basalt edges
zippers with faces
sunrise

through the trunks of three palm trees
past a gnarled root berm
over mango trees
we are windward side
haze lifts

on the water
a freighter is berthed
waiting for port
past the mountain rim
reflections on water
show the red of the ship

even here at home
beyond the tallest maple in the park
above the cavernous freeway
sun opens its palm
catches a puff of lavender gray
radiance grows

flecks of gold shine in hazel eyes
light arrives

TONNIE RICHMOND

GANNET

Shaped by the sea, shaped by the fish I seek
my body knows a trick or two, transforms
my land-based bird-shape into perfect spear.
Darwin would be proud of me.
I fold my black-tipped wings so tight
they disappear into my back
as I javelin from the sky.

A thing

      a streak

           a missile

                fierce blue eyes

                      lock onto my prey.

J.S. WATTS

GULL

I am gull,
a curved blade
through yielding air.
These wings clutch
the seas of the world,
bringing them to me—
the wide shifting wetness,
slate, blue, green,
switching colours with my moods,
undulating rest
rocking me
when my wings
grow fresh power—
the broad, high sea
of blue, grey, white,
its plumage matching mine,
soaring within its embrace
on wings of wind
exalting me forward—
rich, brown seas
rolling beneath my wings,
rippling with dark earth,
churned offering
by the pitiful flightless,
and the storm-high waves
of mottled votive food
piled for my delight and strength.
I shriek with the pleasure,
my call ripping the air
like beak through flesh,
so all may know me as gull,
god of all seas.

LAUREN K. NIXON

WATER SOUNDS

like walking in the woods. Like days spent rambling on the moor, following quiet music to a thin stream. A river's busy shout.

It sounds like the empty time in the garden centre by Wolseley Bridge in 1998, just before rush hour kicks in. Of trickling pots and fake bamboo canes tipping and emptying like an arrhythmic clock. Like picking out waterlilies while Mum debates the merits of pond liners, dreaming of dragonflies and frogs.

It sounds like the great sighs and gasps of the tide against the shore as it rushes away and then scrambles back to fling itself into the rocks' embrace. It sounds like the hiss of saltwater hitting boulders and becoming spray.

It sounds like a quiet morning by the Wharfe, when the clouds could not decide whether to rain or shine and instead spat grumpily, begetting a gloss of rainbows.

It sounds like rain splattering against a windowpane, curtains drawn and sunlight streaming through, transforming the room into butterscotch.

It sounds like the kettle's huffy little complaints when I move it too soon.

It sounds like the pulse in my ears.

BETH KANELL

Honorable Mention for Lit Shark's May-June 2024 Poem of the Month

RESILIENCE, IN THEORY

"natural areas with facilities provided restorative qualities that would help with the physiological and psychological aspects of coping after a disaster"

widowed

foreseen predicted inevitable
my home's crushed, heart stamped upon, head

a scalp wound, they say, bleeds more

this death

: how can I deny the solace
of walking the back road, the mallard paddling
in the pond on the ridge

while its mate hides, considers nesting
(oh, I know) this tiny pond won't be their long-term place

you were my shelter

now rainstorms sting less, in their way, than
sunshine

illuminating the garden

restoration, like rehabilitation, only comes
with pain

LYNETTE G. ESPOSITO

Frogs on a green leaf

flash their long pink tongues at flies

Like Gods seek nectar.

KB BALLENTINE

DREAMTIME, I WILL SING

The air throbs with cicada song,
    midsummer just past. Listen to the trees.
Night widens and fireflies flare hope
    as dusk-singers lullaby the sun,
mauve painting the sky. Crickets linger
    somewhere in the gloom while heat
lightning simmers its soundless tune.
    Stars scattered like seeds peek
around the rising moon, an invitation
    to follow, to abandon this day, this time.
Let it fade into sound and shadow.

EIGHT:
KINGDOM BY THE SEA

URSULA MCCABE

Honorable Mention for Lit Shark's July-August 2024 Poem of the Month

GARDENING IN ASTORIA

This fishing village leans over
a river's mouth meeting the ocean.
It's a melding of senses out here,
views of cargo ships, plank walkways,
braying seals, and rusted canneries
built for the pink flesh of salmon.

Our noses tilt for smells
of fish, sun baked bricks,
and teriyaki from the farmers market,
Victorian houses line narrow sidewalks.

As you turn around
I snap a shot.
Your smile sits almost as wide
as it did a couple years ago,
before we lost him over a bridge
in another coast town down south.

I reach into myself for the place
that guards his temple of loss,
the place where I find the courage to
be uneasy. I can't fix this.

I stay with it, and finally
something loosens,
inside me I water my garden of tenderness.
What remains must be nurtured.

LORRAINE CAPUTO

ALONG THE STRAND

I arrive to this coastal village
to walk to the end
of its long grey strand
strewn with
golden glints,
to where ancient shells
erode from the cliffs
& mix with modern ones
from this sea.

In past days, strong waves
ripped at this coast.
But today
the ocean is more pacific
yet a bit rough,
crossed currents
foaming upon the beach,

where whimbrels &
oystercatchers
pry open shells
with their beaks,
where multitudes of gulls
huddle into the *arena*
& sandpipers
step lightly upon
those golden glints

LAUREN K. NIXON

TESTAMENT OF THE NAIAD OF LITTLE BECK, BAILDON

This has been my well from before human hands raised it from a spring among the chestnuts and the harebells. This is my garden of rocks and walls, made by chattering, ephemeral things. Their dwellings made in little clusters, they sing while they work—not as prettily as birds, but with less purpose. Just for the joy of voices lifting. These nests are cleared for one much grander, then another much grander again.

I watch over my water—not them, though they drink it, taking this place into their blood. They do not seem to last, these small, gaudy things. Boys sent off to war or drowning, women drowning in their own lungs.

Oh, but how they dream! Of straight lines and angles, octagonal kitchens and palaces of glass. They dream of royalty and billiards and neat rows of tame roses.

They dream of curses, too.

They fall like trees when they make their ends, moss covered, bending back towards the earth, streams flowing through, under.

Water finds a way, sifting the silt of broken things.

GREGG NORMAN

THE OYSTER

Who was first
To reach down
Or dive below the surface
Of the moving blue of sea
To place a hand
On the wrinkled shell
Of an oyster?

Who was first
To take it up and back
To the steady dry of land
To prise it open
Sip the saline liquor
Put tongue and teeth to flesh
Of an oyster?

Who was first
To swallow one
And then another and more
To turn to his mate
And softly say
I have for you this gift
Of an oyster?

GREGG NORMAN

BREAKFAST ON THE BOAT

With some guy named Buddy from Seattle,
a new poolside acquaintance from the resort,
looking for a half day's fishing on the cheap,
cruising the fishermen's beach
in Zihuatenejo for the best rate.
Two young boys in an old boat
offer to take us out for next to nothing
with breakfast on the boat included.
We putt-putt out of the harbor,
sitting amidships under a tattered canvas.
The ocean sparkles and slaps softly
at the intruding wooden hull.
Buddy catches a small black tuna
which the boys carve for bait.
The tuna belly brings me a needlefish
trolled up from the base of a lone rock
jutting out of the blue-green water.
It dances topwater like an angry snake.
Later, when I ask about breakfast,
I'm offered a banana
with a shrug and a boy's shy smile.

MICHAEL SHOEMAKER

CREAM PUFF, LE MAGNIFIQUE

You say that you put vanilla pudding in a cream puff?
I thought this was a misdemeanor or a felony.

Oh, cream puff, what is it about you?
With the first bite, I instantly hear
the first eight measures of Debussy's
Clair de Lune, not from a piano,
but the orchestra's string section.
Doesn't everyone?

Your pillow of puff is your golden crown
and below is a white cream
that could blind the whiteness
of the brightest clouds on a summer's day.
To eat you is like breathing blissfulness.

And so, you see
my roommate fair
I am justified
hucking that tennis ball at you
down the hall
when you made off with
—the last cream puff—so stealthily.

TONNIE RICHMOND

MULL HEAD, DEERNESS 2022

The Mull Head cliffs are bare today
no mallimaks feed their young,
no guano paints the cliffs.
Too quiet. Too empty.

Last year, the cliffs were bustling
with new life; fulmars, guillemots,
solan geese, the inevitable bonxies.

It's two years since our own silent summer,
the one we're trying to forget.
Here, there's a new enemy on the breeze,
invisible, deadly. Birds can't isolate,
practice social distancing.
A lifeless gannet
sloughs around in the shallows.

JIM WOLPER

WETLANDS

Despite the highway roar it smells swampy, the smell I'd smelled watching tadpoles, at a distance far from here and a different time of year. None now.

Birds in the lagoon ignore the noise and flap: goose, heron, ibis. Juncos are too small to see this far away. Kites prefer the sea. The Sun's too high for the lark, or meadowlark. There are no nenes on this continent, but ospreys nest nearby, pulling perch from the quagmire. Red robins abound, and sparrows and tits under the hedges. The very young have learned to fly by now, the weather warmer, they cross the swamp.

Yarrow grows in the liminal zone, a balm, calming, doing its magic.

Eagles pass but do not linger, seeing farther.

DIANA WOODCOCK

DARE NOT BLINK

—for the Great Smoky Mountain National Park

Come away from whatever home
to this temperate mountainous zone,
and settle into the dampness,
the ever-present restless sound
of waterfalls and calls of birds.

> Keep your eyes open wide
> for just one of the Smoky's fifteen
> hundred Black bears, just one
> Pileated woodpecker, one
> Fire Pink. Dare not blink.

You'll miss a common mudpuppy,
a misty vista of depth and color.
Never mind the rain, wind, insects.
In time, you'll grow to respect each
aspect of this place so full of grace—

> this temperate zone's warm tones
> of tree trunks, skeletons of Frazier firs
> sheltering saplings surviving, believed
> resistant to the invasive parasite.
> You'll be observed by every animal,

insect, fish and bird. Silent,
reserved, you'll wonder what
you've done (who you are)
to deserve to be so taken in
by your nonhuman kin.

NINE:
TIME TO GIVE BACK

URSULA MCCABE

TODAY'S MORNING

Question-marks with tails
form long lines against the blue
October sky, traffic sounds husky,
as if the stillness
is thick enough to hold heavy things.

The world is thick with brutality
and yet, a lone sycamore is
a beauty mark in the park.

Russet gold leaves form a halo,
their tips hold onto green, soon
they will be strewn on the ground
brown, but today
I am drawn moth-like
to this tree and its beacon of light.

DOUG VAN HOOSER

Winner of Lit Shark's November 2024 Poem of the Month

VARIATIONS ON 'JOY IS NOT MADE TO BE A CRUMB'

—after Mary Oliver

Spring rain washes away the brown. Magnolia petals
strew the greening grass. Squill whispers tulips and
daffodils are coming. The fresh baked pie of May's

blooms. The dresses peonies model. Goldfinch bliss
slaloming through the thistles. Wind chimes chatter
with the wind, clothes lined sheets snapping. Emerald

stain from fresh cut grass. Dragonfly iridescence. Not
the thorns but the rose's myrrh scent that pricks the nose.
The beats of butterfly wings. The ping pong hoots of two

great horned owls in the moonlit dark. The blue jays'
jabber. The doves' soothing coo. A bullfrog's longing
honk. A beehive's symphony. The waking kiss of morning

glories. A ripe tomato's first bite. A stranger's wave and
nod. An old friend knocking at the door. A melting
strawberry ice cream sunset. The missing mistletoe found.

GTIMOTHY GORDON

NIGHTLIGHT

"Let me wipe it first, it smells of mortality."
—Lear to Gloucester who asks to kiss
his hand (*King Lear*, IV:6).

Step outside under nightlight,
count the stars, if possible,
not by number, name, nobody can,
except maybe the boss,
know them by glow, celestial order,
distance from earthly toehold
in this afterworld where you linger
enrapt in the moment with nothing
to hold you here but actual or artful
starlit clarity, guess why they're here
if not for you, if not for you, for who else then?
their gravity lightening heart-heavy you,
alone, sad, cloaked with guilt and shame,
darkness, dread, despair, this mortal coil.

CAROLYN MARTIN

WHAT A POET DESIRES

Not the Pulitzer, National Book Award,
    the *New York Times Best Seller* list,
        pages in the *New Yorker* and *Poet Lore*.

Nor a panel seat with Ava, Billy, and Jericho,
    dazzling rapt audiences with strategies
        perfected in a dozen dazzling poems.

Nor a Perrier sans ice that waits when she walks
    into an Oprah interview to chat about wars
        raging over her sixth manuscript.

Notoriety exhausts, she knows herself well enough
    to know, so she delights in applause when taking
        out the trash and picking up the mail.

When writing a poem-a-week satisfies
    and one *yes* out of fifteen *sends* feels as right
        as walks around the neighborhood to gather

entanglements like the holly berried in Cyprus trees,
    rampant squirrels bickering with Steller's jays,
        and a yellow lab snookered by a stray black cat.

So tonight, when the local laureate riles up
    an adoring crowd, she'll lounge in the back row,
        nodding/smiling/taking a few iambic notes.

NOLAND BLAIN

LIOCONCHA HIEROGLYPHICA

So the ocean tries to speak up
    at last. One day I find you impossibly
        swept to Jupiter Beach, Florida, wet sand
caked across the ridges of your skin.
    For a love letter, you could have chosen
        a more attractive color: peroxide-brown inktails
comma your smooth body,
    like a speech bubble carved
        from a whalebone hunk. Then again,
it isn't so weird for a message
    in a bottle to pop up like a mythical
        hand out of a strange pool, worded
by mystery. Who knows how
    you wormholed through
        the undersea tunnels of the world-wide
waterways, sleeping in
    the salty bellies of whale
        and whalers' net, just to wash up
here: an uncorked
    wedding invite, with the ink
        still smelly, rum-sweet from a pirate
to the father of his mermaid
    bride—if only I could read your
        impenetrable handwriting. An octopus wrote you,
or Godzilla. Whatever ancient city
    you escaped from, whatever dialect
        worked its little ideograms into thumbsized font, I
would like to know
    how to respond to a call
        from a clam old as water.
For instance, is this a booty call?
    Should I bring a toothbrush?
        Are you the relationship type?

DIANA WOODCOCK

KELP FOREST

*—for the Shinnecock kelp farmers,
coastal eastern Long Island, New York*

"... with [kelp] destruction, the numerous
species would soon perish ... and [humans]
... perhaps cease to exist."
—Charles Darwin, 1834

It all begins once summer ends—
threads of baby kelp are spun onto
a synthetic-blend string, then onto
sections of PVC pipe that then are placed
in hatchery tanks. Then daily the team
of women—six intergenerational
Shinnecock women—feed the kelp,
change the tank water, monitor
algal growth and water quality.

December, outplanting begins.
The women enter the water at low
tide to wind the kelp threads onto
anchored rope while prayer and hope
are woven into the work. Let Gaia be on
their side—winds, weather and tide.

Finally, one day in May, they return
to harvest the mature kelp—
800 feet in 2020, 7,000 in 2023.

This is about how six activist
women can turn the tide to honor

their heritage by cultivating sugar
kelp (*Saccharina latissima*) in
Shinnecock Bay.

This is about the sacred connection
to one Protist 32 million years old,
and if the whole truth be told,
about the *kelp highway*—northeast
Asia to the Americas, a linear forest
ecosystem for early maritime peoples.

This is about indigenous coastal tribes
and how they survived for millenia
depending on kelp for shelter and nutrition,
healing and ritual. This is about modern
science proving the beneficial
qualities of kelp—Phlorotannins,
Fucoidans and Fucoxanthins.

This is about man's obligation to
restore the balance, to rectify
the damage caused by dumping/
pumping into the waters untreated
septic waster and chemical fertilizer
runoff. Already the scallop population
has collapsed. But thank Gaia six women
hatched a plan to protect their land
and waters from relentless development.

Praise be to the brave, outspoken ones—
these women of an ancient tribe,
displaced, confined now to nine
hundred acres on a narrow peninsula
projected to be underwater in twenty-
five years—six women who've moved
beyond their fears to recreate
        a kelp kingdom.

THANK YOU FOR READING

ACKNOWLEDGMENTS

Thank you to the publications in which some of these works previously appeared. We appreciate your hard work in getting these pieces out into the world, and we're thrilled to have had the opportunity to share them again.

These entries are organized alphabetically by the contributor's last name and may vary slightly from their previous publication:

"Lost" by Roy Adams was previously publised in William Henry Drummond Poetry Contest Anthology, Cobalt, Ontario, 2016.

"Poem on a Few Lines of Billy Collins's *Whale Day*" by D.C. Buschmann was First published Thursday Poems by Carmel Poets, 2023.

"Pain is a Shark" by Christa Fairbrother was previously published in *MockingHeart Review V.9 #2*.

"Piglet Squid" by Christa Fairbrother was previously published in *HoneyGuide #7*.

"Beached" by Janina Aza Karpinska reviously appeared in February 2019, in Isacoustic magazine, which no longer accepts submissions.

"Bull Male, Sleeping" by Abigail Ottley was included in the 'On the Buses' series, following the Guernsey Literary Festival 2019, and was one of the poems that appeared on Guernsey buses following the Guernsey Literary.

"Turning Turle" by Abigail Ottley was included in the series, Poetry for Mental Health, April, 2024,

"Gull" by J.S. Watts was first published in *Seventh Quarry*, February 2018, and was subsequently published in *The Submerged Sea* by J.S.Watts, 2018.

Doug Van Hooser's "Variations on 'Joy is not made to be a crumb'" is in response to Mary Oliver's poem, "Don't Hesitate."

"Whose Lake Is This" by Michael Zahn is a beautiful play on Robert Frost's "Stopping by Woods on a Snowy Evening."

ABOUT OUR CONTRIBUTORS

Thank you to all of our lovely, imaginative contributors in Issue 8! Here's more about each of them and where to find them.

S. ABDULWASI'H OLAITAN—he/him—Poetry
S. Abdulwasi'h Olaitan is a Nigerian introverted poet and essayist. He writes from a hole 54 kilometers away from Kwara State. He is deeply devoted to God and lover of his parents. He's the author of the longlisted chapbook "Life, An Objet D'art" (Arting Arena Poetry Chapbook Prize 2023) and was a finalist for Chukwuemeka Akachi prize (2024). His works can be found in *Believeau Books, Bare Hill Review, UGR, The Graveyard Zine, Arts Lounge, OPA, Avant Appalachia Ezine, Ta Adesa Magazine, Wordsmpire magazine, Shooting Star Magazine*, and elsewhere.

  Facebook: S Abdulwasi'h Olaitan
  Twitter: S. Abdulwasi'h Olaitan
  Instagram: S. Abdulwasi'h Olaitan

KIKI ADAMS—she/her—Poetry
Kiki Adams is fascinated with the structure and patterns of language. She explores these patterns in her professional life as a linguist, but has also been writing poetry since she was a child. She studied linguistics, psychology, and poetry in her hometown

at the University of Texas at Austin, and now lives in Montreal, Canada. This year, her work has been published in *Aureation Zine, the engine(idling, The Dionysian Public Library*, and *Paddler Press*. When not spending time with words, she can be found out in nature or practicing aerial circus gymnastics.

ROY ADAMS—he/him—Poetry

After a rewarding career as a professor of labour studies, Roy J. Adams (He/Him) resumed the literary career he had begun as a teenager. Since 2010, his creative work has appeared in literary magazines in several countries, including Canada, U.S., U.K., Ireland, India, and Australia. He is the author of *Critical Mass*, a full book of poetry, and the chapbook, *Bebop at Beau's Caboose*. He is a full member of the League of Canadian Poets.

EDWARD AHERN—he/him—Poetry

Ed Ahern resumed writing after forty odd years in foreign intelligence and international sales. He's had over four hundred fifty stories and poems published so far, and eight books. Ed works the other side of writing at *Bewildering Stories*, where he sits on the review board and manages a posse of eight review editors. You can find him on social media under various names: @bottomstripper on Twitter, @edwardahern1860 on Instagram, and /EdAhern73 on Facebook.

LISA NANETTE ALLENDER—she/her—Poetry

Lisa is thrilled to have "Gulf Shores" included in the "Shark Week" issue of *Lit Shark*! Lisa grew up in the Tampa Bay Area and moved to Atlanta after attending USF, and working towards a BA in Theatre Arts, Performance. Since moving to Atlanta, Lisa has enjoyed graduate-level philosophy classes taught by Emory PhD candidates, and has enrolled in Writing Workshops at Indiana University under the tutelage of the late, great poet Maureen Seaton, and at the Palm Beach Poetry Festival, Lisa studied under poet/memoirist/artist Molly Peacock. Lisa is happy to be working again with accomplished poet/memoirist, Cecilia Woloch, as Lisa considers Cecilia her (Wo)-Mentor.

    She is an actor and is represented by the Jana VanDyke

Agency in Atlanta. Lisa is widely published in various magazines and journals. She won First Prize for her sonnet, "Home," in the annual Memorial Poetry Prize offered by John's Creek Poetry Group, in 2022. The judge was poet Danielle Hanson.

    Lisa loves her husband, and entire family, including two shepherd-husky-pittie rescues, Ace and Zelda. She supports rescue work for animals, homeless humans, and is an advocate for LGBTQI+, as well as a volunteer with a peace and social justice group.

    Lisa's new website is www.lisananetteallender.com, and she is launching a foodie blog soon called, "Cake and Read It, Too," while will include cake recipes, many of them Gluten-Free and/or Vegan.

KB BALLENTINE—she/her—Poetry
KB Ballentine's eighth collection, *Spirit of Wild*, launched in March with Blue Light Press. Her earlier books can be found with Iris Press, Blue Light Press, Middle Creek Publishing, and Celtic Cat Publishing. Published in *North Dakota Quarterly, Atlanta Review and Haight-Ashbury Literary Journal*, and others, her work also appears in anthologies including *I Heard a Cardinal Sing* (2022), *The Strategic Poet* (2021), *Pandemic Evolution* (2021), and *Carrying the Branch: Poets in Search of Peace* (2017). Learn more at www.kbballentine.com.

NOLAND BLAIN—he/they—Poetry
Noland Blain (he/they) is a writer and archaeologist from Jacksonville, FL. They are inspired by their love of history, folklore, and the landscape of the American South. They most recently excavated near Siena, Italy, at the site of a Medieval castle built over a Roman bath. Their poetry has appeared or is forthcoming in *SAPIENS, Funicular Magazine, The Roadrunner Review, The Kudzu Review*, and elsewhere.

    Find them on Instagram: @_landless.

DUSTIN BROWN—he/him—Poetry
Dustin P. Brown has a BA in creative writing from Western Michigan University. He was also a fiction reading intern at

Third Coast Magazine and an editorial intern at New Issues Poetry & Prose. These days he lives in Spain working as a freelance editor, writes, and drinks delicious wine. He has poetry published at *Hawaii Pacific Review, Poetry Quarterly, Coe Review, Hollins Critic, Punchnel's, Falling Star Magazine, Waterhouse Review, Third Wednesday*, among others.

D.C. BUSCHMANN—she/her—Poetry

D.C. Buschmann lives in Carmel, Indiana. She is a former teacher, the retired assistant editor of two NW Indiana magazines, and editor of several books. Her first collection of poems, *Nature: Human and Otherwise*, was published in February 2021. She is the founder of Carmel Poetry Group and editor and publisher of Edmund F. Byrne's *My Life Poetically and Thursday Poems*. Her work appears in journals and anthologies internationally, including *AUIS Literary Journal, Tipton Poetry Journal, San Pedro Review, Rat's Ass Review, So it Goes Literary Journal, The Hong Kong Review*, and a forthcoming poem in Nerve Cowboy's editors' pick of the best from 2012-2022.

LORRAINE CAPUTO—she/her—Poetry and Prose

Wandering troubadour Lorraine Caputo's literary works appear in over 400 journals on six continents, and 24 collections of poetry– including *In the Jaguar Valley* (dancing girl press, 2023) and *Santa Marta Ayres* (Origami Poems Project, 2024). She also authors travel narratives, articles and guidebooks. Her writing has been honored by the Parliamentary Poet Laureate of Canada (2011), and nominated for the Best of the Net and the Pushcart Prize. Caputo has done literary readings from Alaska to the Patagonia. She journeys through Latin America with her faithful knapsack Rocinante, listening to the voices of the pueblos and Earth.

    Facebook.com/lorrainecaputo.wanderer
    Website: https://latinamericawanderer.wordpress.com

NICKY CARTER—she/her—Poetry

Nicky is a new poet based in Liverpool. She has worked as an NHS nurse and doctor for forty years and began writing when she retired fully in 2021. Her first pamphlet, *The Ghosts of A and E*, published in September 2024 by Yaffle's Nest, is inspired by the voices of patients and colleagues. She has also had poems published in Journals including *Acumen, Black Nore, Dawntreader, London Grip,* and *Step Away,* and Competition Anthologies *Hippocrates Initiative 2022* (Third Prize and Commended) and Yaffle's *Whirlagust* (Commended 2022 and 2023).

MEGAN CARTWRIGHT—she/her—Poetry
Megan Cartwright (she/her) is an Australian poet and college Literature teacher. Her work has featured print and online in journals and magazines including *Barrelhouse, Contemporary Verse 2, Cordite Poetry Review* and *Verandah*.

ALAN COHEN—he/him—Poetry
Alan Cohen's first publication as a poet was in the PTA Newsletter when he was 10 years old. He attended Vassar College (with a BA in English) and University of California at Davis Medical School, and did his internship in Boston and his residency in Hawaii. He was then a Primary Care physician, teacher, and Chief of Primary Care at the VA, first in Fresno, CA., and later in Roseburg, OR. He now lives with his wife of 44 years in Eugene, OR.

DALE E. COTTINGHAM—he/him—Poetry
Dale Cottingham has published poems and reviews of poetry collections in many journals, including *Prairie Schooner, Ashville Poetry Review,* and *Rain Taxi*. He is a Pushcart Nominee, a Best of Net Nominee, the winner of the 2019 New Millennium Award for Poem of the Year and was a finalist in the 2022 Great Midwest Poetry Contest. His debut volume of poems launched in April, 2023. He lives in Edmond, Oklahoma.

ZENIA DEHAVEN—they/them—Prose
Zenia deHaven (they/them) is a queer writer from Virginia. They are a graduate student in Emerson College's Popular Fiction Writing and Publishing program. They graduated from Virginia Tech with a double major in Creative Writing and Professional and Technical Writing. Their work is published or forthcoming in *Fruitslice, Page Turner Magazine,* and *SIEVA Magazine*. When they're not

writing, they enjoy group exercise classes, video games, and giving their dogs scritches.

    Instagram: @zeniadehaven_
    Linktree; @zeniadehaven.

DAVID DEPHY – he/him – Poetry

David Dephy (he/him) (pronounced as "DAY-vid DE-fee"), is an American award-winning poet and novelist. The founder of Poetry Orchestra. Poet-in-Residence for Brownstone Poets 2024. His poem, "A Sense of Purpose," is going to the Moon by The Lunar Codex, NASA, and Brick Street Poetry in 2024. He is named as "A Literature Luminary" by Bowery Poetry, "Stellar Poet" by Voices of Poetry, "Incomparable Poet" by Statorec, "Brilliant Grace" by Headline Poetry & Press and "Extremely Unique Poetic Voice" by Cultural Daily. He was exiled from his native country of Georgia in 2017 and was granted political asylum in the USA immediately and indefinitely. His family, beloved wife and 9-year-old son joined him in the U.S. after 6 years of exile in 2023. He lives and works in New York City.

CHRISTIANA DOUCETTE – she/her – Poetry

Christiana Doucette builds miniatures in the evenings, because attention to detail makes scenes come alive in beautiful ways. She brings the same attention to details that create emotional resonance in her poetry. She's judged poetry for San Diego Writer's Festival 2022-2024. She is the recipient of the 2024 Kay Yoder Scholarship for American History. Leslie Zampetti [*Open Book Literary*] represents her full-length works. Read her recent/forthcoming poetry in *Rattle, One Art, County Lines, Little Thoughts Press, Boats Against the Current,* and *Wild Peach.*

    Website: https://christianadoucette.wordpress.com
    BlueSky: https://bsky.app/profile/doucette515.bsky.social

CAROL EDWARDS — she/her — Poetry

Carol Edwards is a northern California native transplanted to southern Arizona. She grew up reading fantasy and classic novels, climbing trees, and acquiring frequent grass stains. She currently enjoys a coffee addiction and raising her succulent army. Her favorite shark is the whale shark.

Her poetry has been published in numerous publications, both online and print, including *Space & Time, Uproar* literary blog, Southern Arizona Press, White Stag Publishing, *The Post Grad Journal, Written Tales Magazine*, and *The Wild Word*, and is forthcoming in Black Spot Books. Her debut poetry collection, *The World Eats Love*, released on April 25, 2023 from The Ravens Quoth Press.

Instagram: @practicallypoetical
Twitter/X and FB: @practicallypoet
Website: www.practicallypoetical.wordpress.com

LYNETTE G. ESPOSITO—she/her—Poetry
Lynette G. Esposito, MA Rutgers, has been published in *North of Oxford, Poetry Quarterly, Front Porch, Deep Overstock, Reader's Digest, Self, Fox Chase Review*, and others. She is mostly a poet but also a cat lover. She was married to Attilio J. Esposito and lives in Southern NJ.

CHRISTA FAIRBROTHER—she/her—Poetry
Christa Fairbrother (she/her), MA, is the current poet laureate of Gulfport, Florida. Her poetry has appeared in *Arc Poetry, Pleiades*, and *Salamander*. She's been a finalist for The Pangea Prize, The Prose Poem Competition, The Leslie McGrath Poetry Prize, and nominated for a Pushcart Prize. She's had residencies with the Sundress Academy for the Arts, the Bethany Arts Community, and her chapbook, Chronically Walking, was a finalist for the Kari Ann Flickinger Memorial Prize. Water Yoga (Singing Dragon, 2022), her nonfiction book, won medals from the Nautilus Book Awards and the Florida Writers Association.

Connect with her: www.christafairbrotherwrites.com
Instagram: @christafairbrotherwrites

ISAAC FOX—he/him—Poetry
Isaac Fox plays the clarinet and guitar, makes weird little books, and spends as much time as possible outside. His work has previously appeared in *Bending Genres, Tiny Molecules*, and *A Velvet Giant*, among other publications. Isaac is a co-editor of Shelf

Fungus Press, alongside Abbie Hoffer. You can find him on Twitter at @isaac_k_fox.

> Twitter/X: @isaac_k_fox
> Website: https://isaacfox280.wixsite.com/writing

ANNETTE GAGLIARDI—she/her—Poetry

Annette Gagliardi looks at the dimly tinted shadows and morphed illusions that becomes life and finds illumination. She sees what others do not and grasps the fruit hiding there, then squeezes all the juice that life has to offer and serves it up as poetry—or jelly, depending on the day. Her work has appeared in many literary journals in Canada, England and the USA, including *Motherwell, St. Paul Almanac, Wisconsin Review, American Diversity Report, Origami Poems Project, Amethyst Review, Door IS A Jar, Trouble Among the Stars, Sylvia Magazine, Lit Shark*, and others. Gagliardi's first poetry collection, titled: *A Short Supply of Viability*. In addition, her first historical fiction, titled: *Ponderosa Pines: Days of the Deadwood Forest Fire* were both published in 2022 which won the PenCraft Book Award for Fall, 2023.

> Website: https://annette-gagliardi.com
> Facebook: https://www.facebook.com/annette.gagliardi
> Instagram: @gagliardiannette
> Twitter (X): @annetteJGag
> LinkedIn: linkedin.com/in/annette-gagliardi-a929b7102/

GTIMOTHY GORDON—he/him—Poetry

GTimothy Gordon divides lives among New Mexico/Texas borderland Chihuahuan Desert Southwest Organ Mountains, Asia, and, if the cash-money (as the 'aughts were wont to say) holds out, Europe.

Dream Wind was published in 2020 (Spirit-of-the-Ram Press) followed by *Ground of This Blue Earth* (Mellen Press), and *Everything Speaking Chinese* was awarded the RIVERSTONE Poetry Prize (AZ). His work has appeared in *AGNI, American Literary Review, Cincinnati Poetry Review, Mississippi Review, New York Quarterly, RHINO, Sonora Review*, and *Texas Observer*, and several were nominated for Pushcarts and the Best of the Net. *Empty* was published in January 2024 (Cyberwit Press), and *Blue*

Business was just accepted by Cyberwit Press to be published in Fall-Winter 2024!

BETH KANELL—she/her—Poetry
Beth Kanell lives in northeastern Vermont among rivers, rocks, and a lot of writers. Her poems seek comfortable seats in small well-lit places, including *Lilith Magazine, The Comstock Review, Gyroscope Review, The Post-Grad Journal, Does It Have Pockets?, Anti-Heroin Chic, Ritualwell, Persimmon Tree, Northwind Treasury,* and *Rise Up Review.* Find her memoirs on *Medium,* and her reviews at the *New York Journal of Books* and *Historical Novels Review.* She also writes feature articles, short stories, and novels, recently *This Ardent Flame* and *The Bitter and the Sweet.*
  Website: https://bethkanell.blogspot.com
  Medium: https://bethkanell.medium.com
  Facebook: https://www.facebook.com/BethKanellBooks

JANINA AZA KARPINSKA—she/her—Poetry
Janina Aza Karpinska is an Artist-Poet, fortunate to live near the sea on the south coast of England, which provides a wealth of material for creative arts and poetry. Fortunate, also to have completed and achieved an M.A. in Creative Writing & Personal Development (with Merit), at Sussex University, before the course was dropped from the syllabus to make way for a business department. Her poetry has appeared in: *Ekphrastic Review; Magma; London Reader; Sein und Werd; Cold Signal,* and *Raising the Fifth* among others.

PETER KAY—he/him—Poetry
Peter Kay was born in Heywood, 1950. and now lives in Burton-in-Kendal. He is an author, writer and poet. His published works include two travel memoirs: *A Pennine Way Odyssey* (self-published 2012) and *Show Me The Way to Santiago* (Curious Cat Books 2020), a fictional story, *A Very Alternative Coast to Coast* (Curious Cat Books 2022) and an illustrated Children's Book, *The Owl & The Mole,* (published by Ingram Spark in 2023). He has written and performed poetry for the past 7 years and is currently working on his first poetry

pamphlet, which is to be published by Yaffle Press in Spring 2025. He has had 13 poems included in various anthologies or on-line. He is also currently writing a murder mystery, set in 1930's Yorkshire and ghost writing the Autobiography of a Congolese refugee RAP star.

HELGA KIDDER—she/her—Poetry
Helga Kidder lives in the Tennessee hills with her husband. She loves to look on nature and find the connection to her surroundings. Her poems have recently been published in *Bloodroot, Salvation South, Kakalak,* and others. She has five collections of poetry. Her fifth collection, *Learning Curve,* includes poems about immigration and assimilation.

BETH MARQUEZ—she/her—Poetry
Beth Marquez has recent or upcoming publications in *Cathexis, October Hill, Spillway,* and the *Like a Girl* anthology from Lucid Moose Press, which nominated her poem, "Shedding," for a Pushcart Prize. She is a 2017 Pink Door Fellow and holds three mathematics degrees. She is a freelance statistician, poet, and singer-songwriter residing in Altadena, California.

CAROLYN MARTIN—she/her—Poetry
Blissfully retired in Clackamas, Oregon, Carolyn Martin is a lover of gardening and snorkeling, feral cats and backyard birds, writing, and photography. Since the only poem she wrote in high school was red-penciled "extremely maudlin," she is amazed she has continued to write. Her poems have appeared in more than 175 journals throughout North America, Australia, and the UK, and her latest collection, *It's in the Cards,* was just released by Kelsay Books. See more at www.carolynmartinpoet.com

JULIAN MATTHEWS—he/him—Fiction
Julian Matthews is a mixed-race minority poet and writer from Malaysia, published in *Lit Shark, The American Journal of Poetry, Beltway Poetry Quarterly, Lothlorien Poetry Journal, Live Encounters,* and *New Verse News,* among other journals and anthologies. He stumbled upon a creative writing workshop by

accident in 2017. That happy accident has turned into a rabid compulsion. He is still extricating himself from "the crash."

URSULA MCCABE—she/her—Poetry
Ursula McCabe lives in Portland Oregon where the ocean is not too far away. Her poet father, Robert Huff, taught at Western Washington State University till his death in 1993. Ursula's poems can be seen in *Piker Press, Bluebird World, The Ekphrastic Review, Lit Shark Magazine*, The Wee Sparrow Poetry Press, and others.

CARLIN MCCARTHY—she/her—Photography
Carlin McCarthy is a journalist and photographer out of Brooklyn, NY. Her photography has been published in *Chaotic Merge Magazine*, Pile Press, and *Healthline Zine*, among others. She's interested in capturing the everyday as cinematic and finding frames that make her say, "oh, that's a good shot."
    Website: https://carlinmccarthy.com/
    Instagram: @carlin.mccarthy

LAUREN K. NIXON—she/her—Poetry and Fiction
An ex-archaeologist who swapped the past for the present, Lauren K. Nixon is the author of numerous short stories, *The Fox and the Fool, Mayflies, The Last Human Getaway* and *The House of Vines*, along with poetry collections (including *Wild Daughter, Marry Your Chameleon* and *umbel*.). She has also written two plays – one even on purpose!

    Her poems appear in *Rhubarb: Seconds, Ekphrastic Review, The Lake, Apricot Press, Dream Catcher, The Dawntreader, Reach*, and *The Black Nore Review*, along with several collections by *The Superstars*. When she's not writing, she can be found pootling around the garden or library, researching weird stuff, making miniatures, annoying the cats, and playing board games.
    Website: www.laurenknixon.com

GREGG NORMAN—he/him—Poetry
Gregg Norman lives in a lakeside cottage in Manitoba, Canada, with his wife and a small dog who runs the place. His work has been placed with *Lothlorien Poetry Journal, Dark Winter Literary*

Magazine, *Horror Sleaze Trash*, *The Littoral Magazine*, *Adelaide Literary Magazine*, *Suburban Witchcraft*, *Borderless Journal*, and many more publications in Canada, USA, UK, Australia, and India.

ABIGAIL OTTLEY—she/her—Poetry

Abigail Ottley's poetry and short fiction has been widely published in magazines, journals, and anthologies. This year, she placed second in the Plaza Prose Poem Competition judged by Carrie Etter, and she was the winner of the Wildfire 150 Flash Competition for the second year running. Commended in both the Welshpool and *What We Inherit From Water* competitions, she is a member of Cornwall's all-female Mor Poet Collective. Her debut collection will be published by Yaffle in the spring of 2025. Abigail was born into a tribe of Londoners and was raised in Essex but, having originally moved to Cornwall to take up a teaching post, is now based in Penzance.

You can find her at "Abigail Elizabeth Ottley" on Facebook and Instagram.

CATHERINE PUMA—she/they—Poetry

Catherine Puma (she/they) is a member of the Arlington Writers Group and the Poetry Society of Virginia. When she's not consulting the U.S. government on ocean research, she's staring at the birds outside her window with her rescue dogs and writing poetry on the interplay between humanity and nature.

TONNIE RICHMOND—she/her—Poetry

Tonnie Richmond lives in Leeds and loves Orkney and archaeology. She has had poems published by *The Storms, Black Nore, Up!, Dreamcatcher, Dawntreader*, and others and in various anthologies. Her first pamphlet (poetry chapbook), *Rear-view Mirror*, was published Yaffle's Nest in November 2023.

RIE SHERIDAN ROSE—she/her—Poetry and Prose

Rie Sheridan Rose multitasks. A lot. Her short stories appear in numerous anthologies, including *Nightmare Stalkers* and *Dream Walkers: Vols 1 and 2*, and *Killing It Softly*. She has authored twelve novels, six poetry chapbooks, and lyrics for dozens of songs.

Find more info on www.riewriter.com.

MICHELE RULE — she/her — Poetry

Michele Rule (she/her) is a disabled writer from Kelowna BC, with a special interested in the topic of chronic illness. She is published in *Five Minute Lit, Spillwords, WordCityLit, Poetry Pause* and the anthologies *Chicken Soup for the Soul* and *To Live Here*, among others. Michele won First Prize in the WCWF 2024 contest. She is an associate member of the League of Canadian Poets and co-edits the Solitary Daisy Haiku Journal. Michele lives in a beautiful garden surrounded by people who love her just the way she is.

  Website: https://MicheleRule.ca

AMBER SAYER — she/her — Prose

Amber is not new to the world of writing, as she is a professional health and fitness writer from Westfield, MA, USA. However, she has recently gotten back into creative writing and is working on a middle-grade novel. As an autistic woman, Amber finds she is better able to communicate her thoughts and feelings through writing.

  LinkedIn: linkedin.com/in/amber-sayer-18633728/
  Instagram: @amber.sayer

MICHAEL SHOEMAKER — he/him — Poetry

Michael Shoemaker lives in Magna, Utah, United States with his wife and son where he enjoys looking out on the waters of the Great Salt Lake every day. His is the author of two poetry/photography *Rocky Mountain Reflections* and *Grasshoppers in the Field*. His poetry has appeared in *The High Window, Littoral Magazine, Sea to Sky Review,* and *Petals of Haiku: An Anthology*, an anthology that is a #1 top Amazon Release. Michael loves to read your poetry as a Reader/Proofreader at *Fireflies' Light: A Journal of Short Poetry*.

MIKE SLUCHINSKI — he/him — Poetry

Mike Sluchinski wanders soft beaches worldwide and even sandbars on the South Saskatchewan river. Most of his work runs ekphrastic and stream of consciousness based on his own experiences. He gratefully acknowledges the Cheryl and Henry Kloppenburg Foundation for their support of the arts. He is very gratefully published by *Lit Shark, Poemeleon, The Ekphrastic*

Review, MMPP (Meow Meow Pow Pow), Kelp Journal, 'the fib review', Eternal Haunted Summer, Syncopation Lit. Journal, South Florida Poetry Journal (SOFLOPOJO), Freefall, and more coming!

MARK STROHSCHEIN — he/him — Poetry

Mark Strohschein is a Washington state poet who resides on Whidbey Island. His poems have appeared in *Flint Hills Review, Bryant Literary Review, Barren Magazine, Lips Poetry Magazine, The Milk House, The Big Windows Review* and in anthologies. Forthcoming work will appear in the *Bards West Poetry Anthology, County Lines*, and *Pictura Journal*. His chapbook, *Cries Across Borders*, a semifinalist for Button Poetry's 2023 chapbook contest, will be published by Main Street Rag in the spring of 2025. His chapbook-length collection, *Sanctuary of Voices*, will be published by Ravenna Press in late 2025 as part of its Triple Series.

       Facebook: www.facebook.com/markstrohschein
       Instagram: @strohscheinmark

MCKENZIE LYNN TOZAN — she/her — Poetry

McKenzie Lynn Tozan is a formerly Midwestern writer, since transplanted to coastal Croatia. She received her MFA in Poetry from Western Michigan and is a published poet, novelist, and the Editor-in-Chief of *Lit Shark Magazine* and *Banned Book Review*. Her poems, essays, and book reviews have been featured in *The Rumpus, Green Mountains Review, Whale Road Review, Rogue Agent, POPSUGAR, Motherly*, and *Encore Magazine*, among others. Her short horror story collection, *What We Find in the Dark*, and her horror novella, *Black As Black*, are both forthcoming from The Shiver Collective in 2024. Find more at www.mckenzielynntozan.com.

DOUG VAN HOOSER — he/him — Poetry

Doug Van Hooser splits his time between suburban Chicago where he uses pseudonyms with baristas, and southern Wisconsin where he enjoys sculling and cycling. His poetry has appeared in numerous publications and has been nominated for the Pushcart Prize and Orison Anthology. He has also published short fiction and had readings of his plays in Chicago.

       Links to his work can be found at dougvanhooser.com.

J.S. WATTS—she/her—Fiction

J.S.Watts is a British poet, short story writer and novelist. Her work appears widely in publications in Britain, Ireland, Canada, Australia, New Zealand and the States and has been broadcast on BBC and Independent Radio. She has edited various magazines and anthologies. J.S. has published nine books—poetry collections, *Cats and Other Myths, Years Ago You Coloured Me*, and *Underword*, plus pamphlets, *The Submerged Sea* and multi-award nominated SF poetry pamphlet, *Songs of Steelyard Sue*. Her novels are *A Darker Moon* (dark fiction) and *Witchlight, Old Light*, and *Elderlight* (all urban paranormal).

See more at her website: https://www.jswatts.co.uk/
Find her on Facebook: www.facebook.com/J.S.Watts.page

JIM WOLPER—he/him—Prose

Jim Wolper taught Math for a century (if you round to the nearest century), was a professional pilot, and is a passionate cook. He writes poetry, fiction, travel pieces, philosophical essays, and technical pieces in Mathematics and in Aviation. His chapbook *Misdirections*, will appear soon from Finishing Line Press. He and his wife live with their corgi near Portland, OR.

X: @DrATP
Instagram: @jimwolper
Substack: jimwolper

CHRIS WOOD—she/her—Poetry

Chris Wood manages numbers by day, spends most evenings cleaning up dog hair from the abundance of love she receives from her fur-babies, and in between, she writes to balance her right brain from her left. She has a bachelor's degree in accounting and works for a REIT. Her work has appeared in several journals and publications, including *Poetry Quarterly, Black Moon Magazine and Salvation South*.

Learn more at chriswoodwriter.com.

DIANA WOODCOCK—she/her—Poetry

Diana Woodcock has authored seven chapbooks and six poetry collections, most recently *Heaven Underfoot* (winner of the 2022 Codhill Press Pauline Uchmanowicz Poetry Award), *Holy Sparks* (2020 Paraclete Press Poetry Award finalist), and *Facing Aridity* (2020 Prism Prize for Climate Literature finalist). A three-time Pushcart Prize nominee and Best of the Net nominee, she received the 2011 Vernice Quebodeaux Pathways Poetry Prize for Women for her debut collection, *Swaying on the Elephant's Shoulders*. Currently teaching at VCUarts Qatar, she holds a PhD in Creative Writing from Lancaster University, where she researched poetry's role in the search for an environmental ethic.

MICHAEL O. ZAHN—he/him—Poetry
Michael O. Zahn lives in Poinciana in Central Florida. His poem, "Volunteer Swim Coach: A Tribute," was a finalist in the 2022 Robert Frost Foundation international competition. The service manager at the Kia dealership in Lake Wales, Florida, has tacked one of Zahn's poems on his corkboard. Born in 1947, Zahn was a reporter at the *Milwaukee Journal*.

SUBMIT TO LIT SHARK OR WRITE FOR US!

Thank you again to everyone who submitted to Issue 8 of *Lit Shark Magazine*. It was honestly such a lovely process, and I'm so grateful for your support and continuing this journey.

If you're interested in submitting your work for consideration at *Lit Shark Magazine*, you'll find the most up to date information on our website: www.litshark.com.

In addition to our general and themed issues of *Lit Shark Magazine*, we also have our paid, monthly **Poem of the Month Contest** and weekly opportunities to submit creative responses to the **writing prompts** we share on our website.

We're also always interested in hearing from potential book reviewers, conservation/sustainability writers, marine biology/ecology writers, and anyone with interesting stories about marine life, whale sightings, swimming with sharks—anything on your heart/in your imagination!

Happy Writing and Happy Submitting, readers, writers, and shark fans—and thanks again for reading Issue 8!

FIN.
(UNTIL ISSUE #9...)

Made in the USA
Columbia, SC
16 January 2025